LARRY SCEURMAN

Coffee in the Morning

A collection of short stories
fragments of life from dreams, fiction, and fantasy

CONNECT with the publisher:
ParisianPhoenix
ParisBirdBooks
angel@parisianphoenix.com

CONNECT with the author:
lvstorytelling.org/live/teller/larry-sceurman/
ParisianPhoenix.com/Larry
larbarstory@gmail.com

Dedicated to the joyful struggle
within the journey of creation.

TABLE OF CONTENTS

DRINK
Coca-Cola
DELICIOUS AND RE...ING

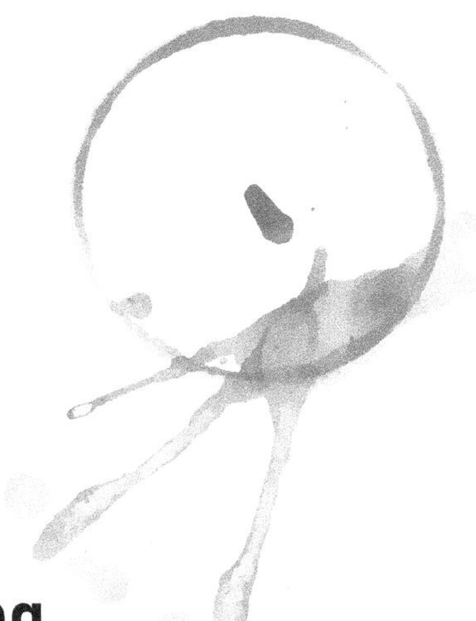

Introduction:
Coffee in the Morning

I like to sit and watch the sunrise, twilight breaking into daylight, a magical time of day. The night sky conceals creative ideas. In rare moments as I sleep, the night sprinkles seeds of a story amongst my dreams. Then, at daybreak, the seeds germinate into creative thoughts.

When I was in my early thirties, sitting at the kitchen table in my boxers with socks on my feet, wearing an old comfortable flannel shirt, a cup of coffee in front of me, and gazing out the back door, I would sit and think about planning my day, planning my future. Sometimes I would write, draw, or paint. Most of the time, I would dream.

I remember my mother sitting at the dining room table looking out the window into the sky enjoying her morning cup of coffee. She spent her coffee time the same way her mother, my Nana, did it. After all the breakfast dishes were cleared away, Nana would sit at the kitchen table with her two pink plastic rollers in her hair and a coffee cup. She would sip her coffee, and gaze into the dining room, and beyond the dining room, into the living room.

It was her time for a cup of coffee, she would say. I think it was the time during which they both planned their day or the next couple of days. Many times, they had a pad of paper next to them and they would write the shopping list, or the store order as they would call it. Sometimes they would write down things that they didn't want to forget and doodle in the margins.

But most of the time, I think they would dream with a cup of coffee. Sipping and dreaming. You see lots of people rushing around with their to-go cups in hand. Not relaxed and sipping their coffee, but in a hurry, gulping the morning cup. I hope that some people get to sip and dream with their cup of coffee, at least for a few minutes.

Over the years, I learned that sipping and dreaming stimulates the creative process. I, like my mother and grandmother, enjoy the morning. Others may do their sipping and dreaming when the sun goes down and yet others, midway in the day. Whatever time one enjoys sipping and dreaming...That is a perfect time.

What you sip is not important. Whether you choose coffee, tea, lemonade, water or wine, the important part remains how you dream, not what or how you sip. What is important is that you don't overdo the sipping and forget about dreaming. The sipping gives you permission to dream. The dreaming is the most important part of the creative process. Dreaming is the threshold to creativity. From creativity emerges the energy for the action and action produces the art. It starts with sipping and dreaming.

As I write this, the sun is coming up on a cold winter's day. I'm sitting at my laptop with slippers on my feet, wearing an old comfortable flannel shirt and I'm sipping coffee and dreaming.

Now today's dreaming is not anything special or spectacular, it is just dreaming. Creativity whispers in my ear. Memories emerge, telling me to save these thoughts on paper. So, I listen...

Our creative thoughts are drops of artistic rain that gather into springs of imagination that run into inventive creeks that merge with rivers of vision that flow into oceans of art. Our work is not just a drop in the ocean, but it is many drops to create an ocean of art.

So, I raise my cup of coffee to you and sip and say, "May you be a sipper and a dreamer. May your creativity flow."

God Bless and Have Fun!

LARRY

The General Store

Mrs. Waterman rolled into the hardware store and placed a blue ball on the counter and said, "What color is this ball?"

"Blue," said Henry.

"I know it's blue, but what color blue? Is it a periwinkle blue or is it more of a cornflower blue? It might even be a slate blue. No, it's too blue for that."

"It's ...racquetball blue," said Henry.

"Henry, I want to match this color blue. I'm painting my big shed out back, it's now a faded avocado green and I think this blue would look very nice. How much paint do you think I would need?"

"If you put on a primer sealer, I think a gallon and a quart would do her."

Hyle's Hardware and General Store sat on Main Street for more than 70 years. Henry's father started the store at the end of World War II and Henry's been running it for the past 30 years.

The bell jingled when the door opened, Henry didn't pay it any mind, but when the door slammed shut his head jerked. John Haas moved with motivation toward the counter. His arms were bent at the elbow, fists clenched and moving back and forth in a mechanical motion. His face was red like a pomegranate, his mustache drooped down into a frown and his eyes burned hot like two automotive fuses.

"I need one of them flat pry bars," said John. "I really screwed up this time."

"Just hold on a minute 'til I take care of Mrs. Waterman," said Henry.

"No," he said. "You don't understand, I locked Lily in the bathroom. I really screwed up."

Henry pointed.

"You'll find them over there along the wall."

"Don't know how I did it. The door shut behind me and it was locked. She's up there howling and throwing things around. Knowing her, she'll be pissing and shitting on the floor just for spite. Where did you say they were?"

Henry pointed again toward the wall. John walked away to find the pry bar, still saying he screwed up. Henry leaned toward Mrs. Waterman.

"Lily is his dog. A black lab that's about as dumb and screwy as this three-inch threaded pipe."

He tapped a piece of pipe on the counter. Mrs. Waterman chuckled and shifted her weight in her wheelchair and started to turn it around while asking Henry where the primer sealer was located. Henry stepped from behind the counter.

"No, no, I can get it for you," he said. "I have to go over to the paint department to mix up this blue for you anyway. Do you need anything else: brushes, scraper, sandpaper?"

Mrs. Waterman gathered her thoughts as if they were hanging on hooks in midair.

"No, I think my nephew has all the tools that are necessary."

She followed Henry. Her wheelchair squeaked like an old, rusty wheelbarrow.

Without turning around or breaking stride, Henry said, "I'll throw in a small can of 3-IN-ONE Oil. Don't worry, Mrs. Waterman. It's on the house."

Just as Mrs. Waterman started to say there was no need for that, the bell jingled at the front door. This time, Henry turned to see who entered the store. Henry looked to Mrs. Waterman.

"It's Buddy Cobb," he said in a low voice.

"Oh," said Mrs. Waterman. "Is that the man that the sign is about?"

"What sign?" Henry asked.

"The sign by your delicious candy bins. It says 'No grazing except for Buddy Cobb.' Is that the Buddy Cobb that the sign speaks about?"

"Yes, that's the man. That is Buddy Cobb."

"I do think it's a humorous sign, but why does he get to graze?"

Henry sighed and looked around before he spoke.

"Well, it's a bit of a long story but the short of it is, Buddy comes in the store a couple or three times a week, not just for the candy. Sometimes he needs something or sometimes he just comes in to chat, but he always takes a little candy.

Sometimes he'll have a handful of jellybeans and eat them right in front of you as you have a conversation and then he walks out the door. Other times he'll grab a fistful of Mary Janes and shove them in his pocket. Yet, other times he just stands there and grazes on some chocolate or has a piece of licorice.

Then at the end of every month, we get an anonymous money order that just says candy on it. The amount of the money order varies from month to month, I guess it's whatever he thinks he owes us for that month. It's been going on for years. It started when my father was here."

Mrs. Waterman shook her head with a laugh.

"How humorously odd."

"Henry, Henry," John Haas called. "What do I owe you for this pry bar?"

"Excuse me, Mrs. Waterman," said Henry as he rushed to the counter. "Lily is in need."

"Look, John, why do you need a pry bar? Can't you open the door with the key?"

"It's one of them old-fashioned doors and the lock needs one of those old-fashioned keys."

"A skeleton key," replied Henry. "Like one of these."

Henry held up a large ring of skeleton keys. He told John that he could take the ring of keys home and try them on his door. He reassured John that one of the keys should fit his lock and that he shouldn't have to pry open the door and go through all that trouble and expense. He could take the pry bar home, too, and if he didn't use it, just bring it back to the store. As John thanked Henry, the bell above the door jingled again.

In walked a young man: mid-twenties, black leather jacket, black tight pants, and purple high-top sneakers. His hair looked like an open book of matches sticking straight up with pink ends. He sniffed and wiped his nose nervously as he scanned the store.

While approaching the counter, he slowly pulled a gun out of his jacket. The pistol seemed awkward in his skinny hand. He gripped it tightly like a clamp on a piece of steel.

"Just came for the money," the young man said in a slow, clear voice. "Nobody will get hurt, I just want the money."

He pointed the gun at John Haas.

"Step away from the counter," the gunman said. "Give me your money."

John brought out an old bi-fold wallet with a rip on the back. He opened it to show that the only money he had was a twenty-dollar bill. The young thief snatched it out of John's hand.

"Lie on the floor," he told John.

John did. The young man turned toward Henry behind the counter, pointing the gun and telling him to give him all the money that's in the cash register. Squeak, squeak. Mrs. Waterman came rolling from the paint department.

"Henry, what is delaying you? I've been waiting..." she said as she cruised the aisle. "Oh my, that boy has a gun!"

"I'm here for the money, Granny," said the robber. "Just get over here and give me whatever is in your purse."

From the candy bins, Buddy Cobb walked slowly toward them with a small brown paper bag in his hand. Out of the corner of his eye, the robber caught a glimpse of Buddy. The robber jerked and stared at Buddy. Buddy offered him the paper bag.

"Would you like some candy? It's pretty damn good candy. From the looks of things, a couple of jellybeans would do you good."

Buddy steadily continued to walk closer while dipping his hand into the brown paper bag and popping small handfuls of jelly beans into his mouth.

"I don't want any of your fucking jellybeans. Just want your money," said the thief. His eyes darted back and forth—from Buddy Cobb to Henry, then he snarled at Henry.

"Get the goddamn money out of the register."

"Have a little patience, young man." Mrs. Waterman said. "Henry is doing the best he can."

"And you, Granny? Hurry up and give me what's in your purse!"

Mrs. Waterman opened the large purse she had in her lap.

"I'm an old lady in a wheelchair. But now..."

She had her arm deep in the purse.

"I'm an old lady in a wheelchair with a gun."

Suddenly, she held a chrome automatic pistol that glistened in the fluorescent light.

"You need to think about this young man," Mrs. Waterman continued. "I am an old woman in a wheelchair, and it would be quite glorious if I were to meet my maker defending myself."

The robber laughed out loud.

"Now you, on the other hand, being the young man that you are, if you were to shoot an old lady in a wheelchair, I'm sure you would get 20 years-to-life. But if I shot you, I most certainly would become a heroine."

"You're not going to shoot me, ya old, crippled bitch," the robber said.

"Yes," Buddy said. "You might want to think this over. Are you sure you don't want some candy?"

"No fucking candy. I'm here for money," said the robber.

Buddy Cobb continued to move forward at a slow pace, munching on jellybeans.

"When I was young, I got in trouble with the law," he said. "A war was going on at the time and sometimes they gave you a choice, jail or the Army. I picked the Army and went to war."

"I don't want to hear your goddamn war story; I just want your fucking money."

"I don't carry money. Put everything on account or I use my charge card," said Buddy.

"That's true," said Henry. "He charges everything."

The young crook looked toward Henry and his gun seemed to look in that direction too. He wiped his nose as if his nervousness was leaking out of him.

"Just open up the cash register and give me the fucking money and I'll be out of here. Then you all can go on with your stupid lives, but now you'll have one hell of a story to tell," the young man said. "For the last time, give me the fucking money."

Buddy Cobb stood a little bit closer to the robber and cleared his throat, as if to say, Excuse me, let's bring the attention over to me now. The thief turned toward Buddy and his gun followed. He glanced at Mrs. Waterman and then stared at Buddy. Once more, he wiped his nose and rubbed his fingers on his black pants, leaving a streak.

"There is one thing that I've learned in my life," said Buddy. "There are two true emotions: love and fear. When you shoot somebody, even in war, there is a ghostly fear that stays with you for the rest of your life."

"It's time for you to shut up, candy man."

The young robber brought the gun up even with his stare...

Bang!

Everyone jumped, everyone but the young robber now lying on the floor. Buddy Cobb quickly removed the gun from the young man's grip.

"Henry, call an ambulance. Call 9-1-1."

John Haas slowly got up from the floor, thinking about his twenty-dollar bill. Henry fumbled with the phone and looked to Mrs. Waterman and asked if she was all right.

A trembling Mrs. Waterman looked at her shiny gun with smoke lingering from the barrel.

"I'm really scared..." she said. "It's that ghostly fear. It's already crawled inside me."

Poems for Pawnbrokers

Letting Go of Guitar Dreams

The newly fallen snow makes the sidewalk slippery.
Looking up and seeing the three gold balls above the door,
Subconsciously I am whispering faith, hope, and charity.
Stepping inside, the array of merchandise floods my vision.
There is a smell of money that fluctuates
Between a sweet fragrance and a sour odor.
My head turns as I hear, "How can I help you?"
A bald-headed man with a kind smile,
Which is draped by a mustache, says,
"Come here, let's see what you have for me."

I place the case on the counter and open it slowly,
"A seventy-two Les Paul, a little worn but sounds great."
Shoving an unlit half cigar in his mouth,
He carefully takes the starburst guitar out of the case.
The kind smile says, "Feels good. Show me her sweet sound."
I plug into the store's amp and deliver a slow Blues.
"What do you need?" is asked.
I try not to look him in the eye,
So I don't show my desperation.
"I was thinking three thousand."
"A question I don't usually ask, but
Why are you parting ways with such a fine guitar?"
"Life played too many wrong notes."
"It looks to me that this guitar has been on tour with some fine musicians.
I will give you two thousand five hundred and loan you a guitar.
I'm not here to steal your dreams,
I like to think I can lend you some hope."
Twenty five 100-dollar bills are placed in my hand,
I can't hold back the smile on my face.
I take a deep breath;
The smell of money is still sweet and bitter.
But faith, hope, and charity are singing a new tune into my ear.

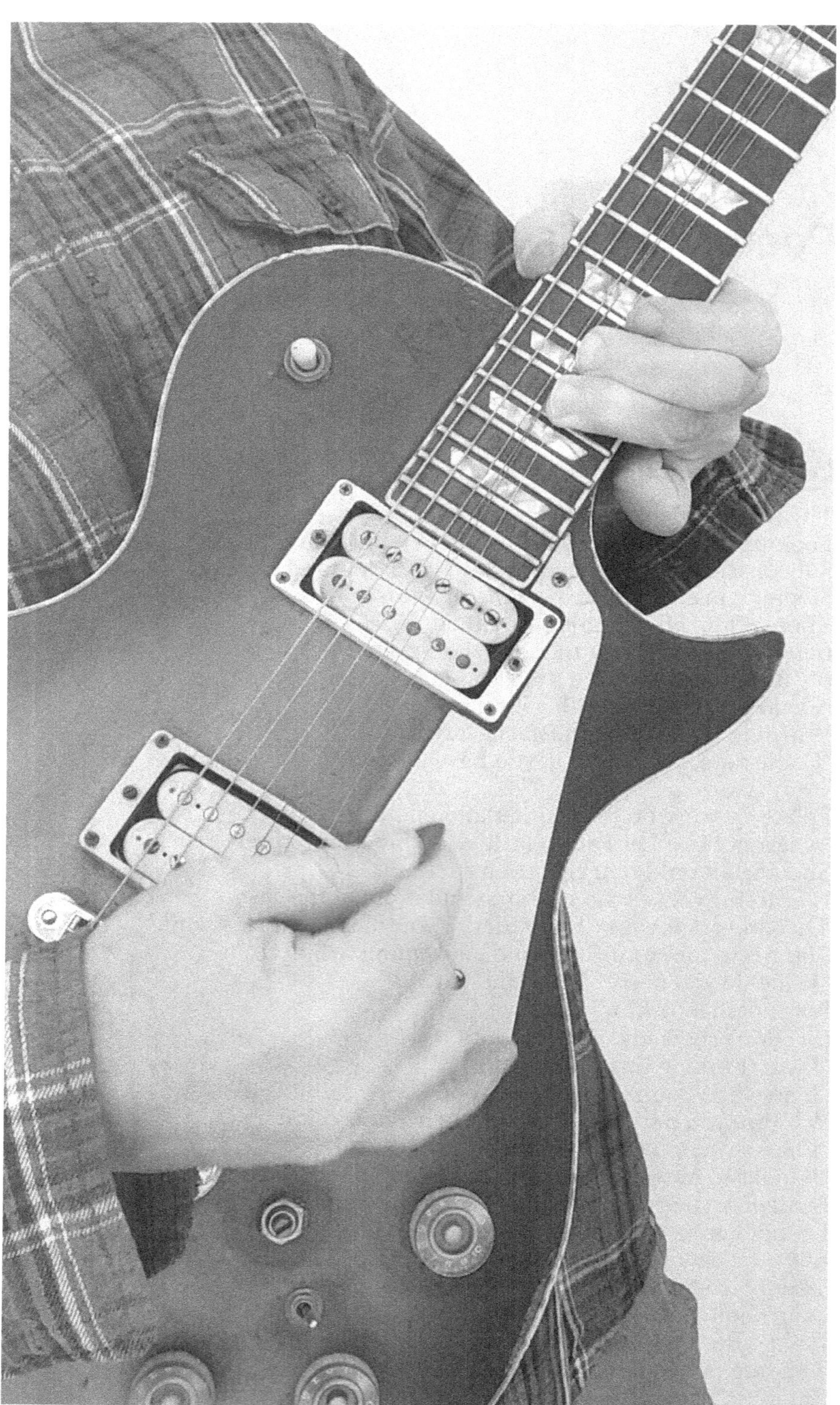

Pawnbroker's Sigh

Snow is falling, it will be a slow night.
To close early and have a drink and a cigar might be a good thing.
I count the cash in the drawer.
The feel of money can be enjoyable or harsh.
Three bells above the door jingle and
I automatically say, "How can I help you?"

There stands a long-haired young man
With a worried look and guitar case in hand.
"Come here, let me see what you have for me."
His graceful hands open the guitar case slow and with care,
"A seventy-two Les Paul."
A look of sincerity says,
"A little worn, but sounds great."

I bite on my cigar and lift the sunburst guitar out of its case.
I can feel the nobility of the instrument,
"Feels good. Show me her sweet sound."
He plugs the Gibson into the amp and
Creates a sound of magnificence and skill.
The slow blues have me hooked;
The guitar may be worth four grand
But I know he will take two.

His body language and the look upon his face
When he plays, tells me he's in love with this guitar.
I ask, "What do you need?"
"I was thinking $3000."
I could set the hook for $2000
And he would take it.
But I sense this kid is different and
I find myself asking the taboo question.
"Why are you parting with such a fine guitar?"

His poetic answer, "Life played too many wrong notes"
Started the wheels in my head turning.
"It looks to me that this guitar has been on tour with some fine musicians."
The young musician nods.
The businessman part of me
Bites harder on my cigar,
as the generous soft touch within me ignores making a buck.
I find myself saying,
"I'll give you two thousand five hundred and loan you a guitar.
I'm not here to steal your dreams,
I like to think I can lend you some hope."
Placing twenty-five $100 bills in his hand feels enjoyable.
And the Big-Hearted Blues plays softly in my ear.

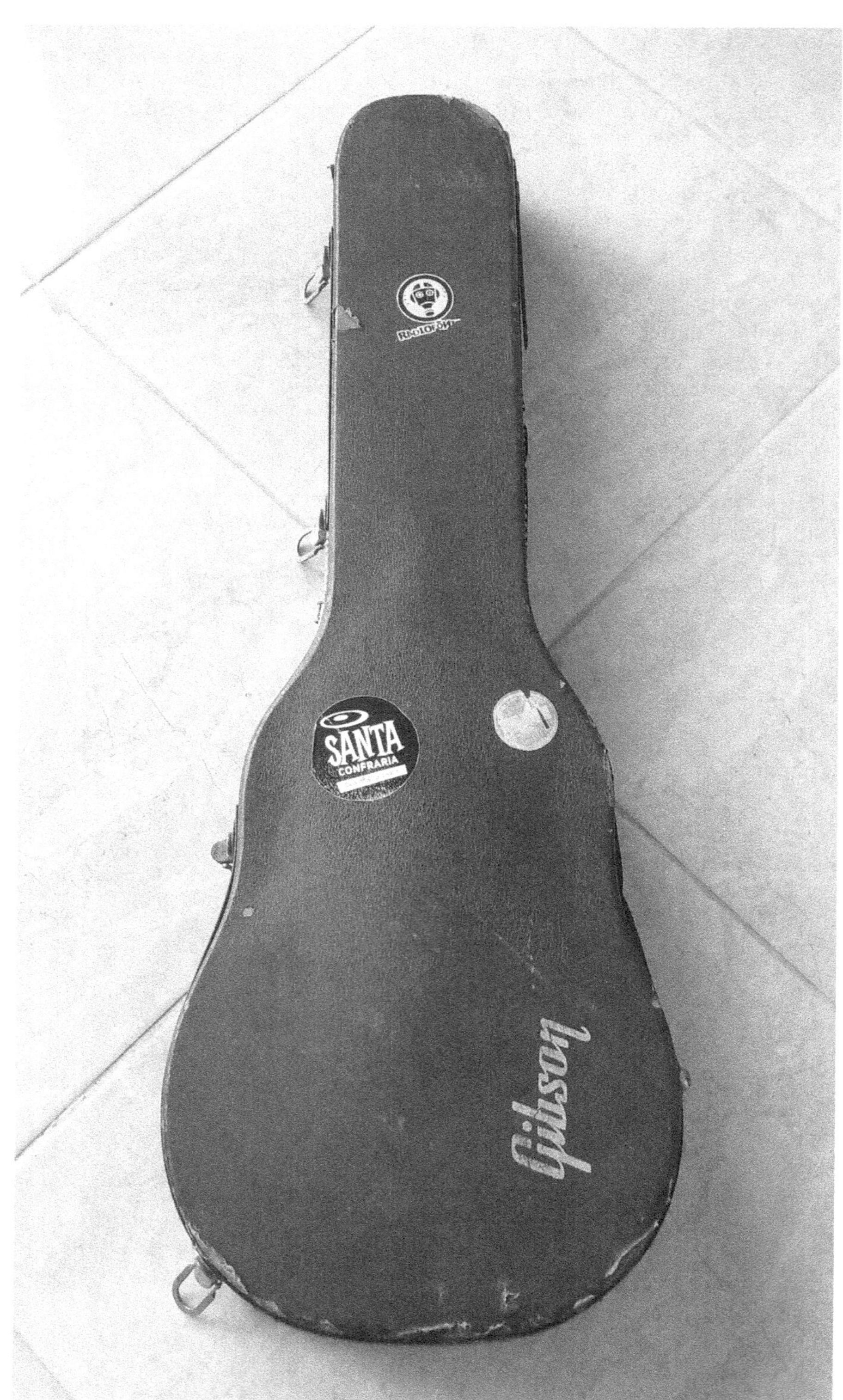

PhotoGram
SANTA
CONFRARIA
Gibson

The Guitar Looks On

I can feel moisture upon my case.
I hear a door open and bells jingle,
A sound that I faintly remember.
There is silence.
Then I hear a muffled voice of curiosity.
I am laid down horizontally and my case is slowly opened.
A face of inquisitiveness is biting on a cigar.
'Oh, please don't let that ash drop on me.'
I hold tight, as unfamiliar fat hands of uncertainty pick me up.
They speak of my age, beauty, and quality.
I'm plugged in and the skilled hands of the Maestro pluck my strings.
A slow soothing melodic sound is produced
Between the agreement of his fingers and my strings.
I can feel the respect, appreciation, and love in his hands.
It is too short. The playing is too short.
Why are you stopping?
I can see money exchanged.
I intuitively know that the Maestro is leaving me.
I ache inside, for yet again I will be in the hands of someone new.
I am placed in the case and the lid closes.
Once more I'm sitting in darkness with faith
...Hoping that charity will grace my strings again.

Editor's note: This story first appeared in The Write Connections: The 2017 Anthology of the Greater Lehigh Valley Writers Group. *That book, and volumes from other years, are still available on Amazon.com. Reprinted with permission and thanks.*

Amnesia Exercise: Breathing Underwater

It is as if I woke up, not from a dream but into a dream. Sitting at the bar, with pencil in hand, staring at what is scribbled on the napkin.

When the tide comes in, we retreat with the backpedaling energy of fear.
When the tide goes out, we advance with the frontward energy of fear.
Somewhere between the tide coming in and the tide going out,
we feel something under our feet— smooth and rough, spiny and rigid.
When we dig it up, we find it is an ancient being,
We must learn to breathe underwater.

What is this tide coming in and tide going out? Fears? Ancient beings and breathing underwater? Did I write this?

Who am I? Where am I? Who's this man waving a sandwich and talking at me?

"I'm telling you. There's an art to making a sandwich. Am I right or wrong? Look...You start with the bread and then you put on the ham, then the cheese, then the mustard. Maybe a little bit of horseradish. More cheese on top of the mustard, then more ham on top of the cheese, and then bread. Hey, am I right or wrong? See, everything is layered on top of each other. That's why you call it a sandwich. Is this a great sandwich or what?"

He takes a bite of his sandwich and starts talking with his mouth full.

"My crazy wife, Helen, she don't know how to make a sandwich! You take peanut butter and jelly. My crazy wife puts jelly on the bread first! I tell her, 'Helen, the peanut butter goes on the bread first, never the jelly.

A good peanut butter and jelly sandwich has peanut butter on each side of the bread and jelly in the middle.' Hey! Tell me. Am I right or wrong?"

I'm sitting here, staring at this man with the big, bushy eyebrows, intense, dark eyes and a big, brown mustache. He's telling me how to make a sandwich. I think I might know him.

At the same time, I look around, searching for clues that will bring me out of this dream. I am wearing a wedding ring. I must be married.

And the bartender seems to know me.

The man with the mustache takes two quick bites of the sandwich. He finishes his beer and puts money on the bar. Then, he speaks to the bartender.

"Sam, you got the best free lunch in town."

He slaps me on the back and once more asks if he was right or wrong. He points to me and tells Sam the bartender to give Steve another drink on him.

"Good luck," he says to me. "We will keep you in our prayers."

He salutes me and walks out.

He called me 'Steve.' Is that my name? Steve? What is this good luck and prayers stuff? I take a sip of my beer. I glance down and see I'm in uniform. My sleeve has two stripes. I'm a corporal. I check my pockets. There must be something in my pockets.

A pack of Lucky's and a book of matches. Huh...There's also a piece of paper. I unfold it. It says, 'Stephen J. Kowalski.'

But that's my father's name, Stephen J. Kowalski. How do I know that's my father's name? I don't know who I am. How could I know who my father is?

I study the orders more carefully. I'm to report to Fort Dix, New Jersey, January 25, 1944, to be assigned to the First Infantry Division in England.

Sam the bartender puts another beer in front of me. I ask him about the guy with the sandwich. He laughs.

"Your Uncle Pete was in rare form today," he says.

He wipes off the bar in front of me and sets down a coaster. A very pretty blonde woman with sparkling blue eyes sits next to me. The bartender winks at me.

"Gotta be on your best behavior now."

Then, he looks to the woman.

"What'll you have, Ann?"

"Oh, I'll have a beer like Steve," says the blonde.

My mind swirls. I can't take my eyes off this woman. Her voice is so familiar and her voice haunts me in a pleasant way. The bartender called her 'Ann.'

"Steve," the blonde woman called Ann says, "I'm glad we got married before you go overseas. We only had two weeks together, but it was a wonderful two weeks. I'm so happy we honeymooned in the city. I felt funny staying at my mom's house with you."

She raises her eyebrows and gives me a smile.

"You know what I mean," she adds. "Now it's time to get the train. I'm not going to cry until I kiss you goodbye."

I'm married to this beautiful woman? This is getting crazier and crazier, but better, too. Then, it hits me. It's her voice. I know that voice and those eyes—those big blue eyes. Her name is Ann.

She's my mom!

She's my mom before she was my mom! The guy with the sandwich was my grandfather's brother, the old guy they called Uncle Pete. Then... I'm my father?

But...I never saw my father. My dad died in World War II. He died on Omaha Beach on D-Day. How could this be?

I was born in September 1944.

How do I know this? I just do.

I look at the orders again. January 25, 1944.

I look back at my mom. Look how much in love she is. Her eyes. Her smile. Even her voice. Everything just pouring out love.

Right now, I'm my father

This beautiful woman is my wife.

This is too bizarre.

Maybe I am breathing underwater.

The Bread Maker

The small country, nestled in between the borders of five larger countries, looked insignificant on a map but was largely well-respected for its fairness and craftsmanship. From clocks and watches, chocolate and lace, computer manufacturing to money handling, it was all superbly done.

There was an old-world work ethic instilled within the people. The people had a priceless value system for doing their best and doing it right.

However, there was a drawback. Though young people were encouraged to expand their horizons and follow their dreams, most people ended up doing what their ancestors did. If your family were carpenters, chances are that you would become a carpenter. If your family were known for watchmaking, most likely watchmaking would become your lot in life.

For most people it was accepted and a joyful way of life. But for some it was a burdensome tradition that choked their creativity and stifled their dreams.

Mila was a free-spirited girl who would say, "I have a brain, I have courage and now I must find my dream."

When she was only sixteen, pottery filled her daydreams.

At eighteen, she stared out the window and dreamed of faraway lands.

At twenty, leaving the family bakery behind, she attended college for psychology. The working of the mind filled her thoughts.

Charities and helping the oppressed came next.

Then, she wrote poetry and played the flute with a folk singer named Riley. Entertaining was hard and tiresome.

So back to school she went, and she met a professor named Philip. He wore round wire-rimmed glasses that framed his love-filled eyes, which added to his charming personality, and he had many books and bottles of wine. He (and philosophy) dominated Mila's state of mind.

Traveling then became the motivation within her heart, bankrolled by a variety of jobs that gave her freedom. She was a secretary in Germany, a silversmith in Spain, an assistant lock-tender in Holland, and she could be a waitress wherever she was.

Mila always could turn to the making of dough when she was short of bread, for baking was her family gift, but bread was not in her dreams.

Mila grew tired of living hand-to-mouth while searching for the future. On a cloudy day, she walked along the river with her thoughts drifting. She came upon a group of people who lived under a bridge.

Mila stood and watched an old woman mixing some dough in a wooden bowl and kneading it into a loaf. The old woman broke off globs of dough from the loaf and rolled them out on a flat rock into foot-long, inch-in-diameter, rope-like pieces.

The old woman carefully wrapped each ribbon of dough in a spiral around a stick and seasoned it with salt and cinnamon. The stick's bark was shaved, giving the stick a white, smooth appearance and it was rubbed with olive oil. Each stick rested against a rock, on an angle pointing up, allowing the dough to hang over a bed of hot coals.

Every five minutes or so, the old woman rotated the sticks until the bread spirals became an even golden brown. When the bread was fully baked, she very carefully slid the finished spiraled bread off and wrapped more dough on each stick, again placing them over the fire.

People started to gather. Some people gave her money for the stick bread. While others traded honey, trinkets, or food. A few sat and talked while eating the stick bread with the old woman.

Mila smiled when the old woman looked at her.

The old woman motioned Mila to sit down next to her. So, she did. The old woman gave her a coil of stick bread and asked her name. Mila felt at peace when she answered. The old woman nodded with approval.

"Mila, good name."

"And what is yours?" asked Mila.

"Rosalee."

"Pretty," Mila said with a smile.

"You like the stick bread?" the old one asked.

"Yes, this is delicious."

"Dip it in the honey or butter. It is better."

Rosalee slowly moved around the campfire turning the sticks of bread.

"I have been making bread on a stick since I was a child."

The glow of the coals made her face red and her long-braided silver hair shine. Her dress was maroon with pink and blue and yellow embroidery on the front, gray dust from the coals clung to the bottom. Her smooth, dark brown boots that peeked from under the hem of her dress gave her balance and stability. Rosalee went on.

"Yes, many years I have been making bread on a stick. I learned from my grandmother. My father's people were travelers and at night we would sit around the campfire eating salted stick bread with honey and butter. There was music and laughter and talk, but us kids would always get some bread and a story and then off to bed."

"Stories? What kind of stories?" asked Mila.

"Romani stories." Rosalee laughed and continued, "Educated people may call them Gypsy folktales, but the real educated people say Romani tales."

"Will you tell me a Romani story?" Mila asked.

Rosalee smiled.

"There was a young Romani fiddler named Vano who was restless. He longed to travel solitary and mingle with the Gadjo, non-Gypsies, to learn and share their music. He was in search of what he called a creative bohemian dream. Then one night he told his sister of his dream. He gave her all his possessions, except the clothes on his back, a knife and his fiddle and bow. He made her promise not to tell of his departure for twenty-four hours. So, he left and traveled to many countries where he found harsh prejudice toward his traveler heritage but also great friendship amongst musicians and artists. So, he played music, drank and ate, philosophized with talk, and lived the life of a troubadour. But he still felt restless.

His uncle, who had taught Vano to play, was also an accomplished woodworker who made elegant instruments. When Vano was young, he had learned basic woodworking skills and how to maintain and repair stringed instruments. One winter in Germany, Vano apprenticed with the master craftsman, Wolfgang, who made well-designed violins. Vano's reasoning for being an apprentice was to stay warm. It was too hard to travel in the severe winter. An apprenticeship was a particularly good way to be creative.

During this time, he not only learned to make violins, but he learned to read music. In his searching for the new, he became blind to the old, but when he stood still the old ways opened his eyes.

He became a composer and blended his Romani roots with modern styles, coming to his bohemian dream by way of his traveler heritage. Vano lived his life by blending the old and the new. He traveled with his family and played music with his friends in the summer. But in the winter, you would find him in the north of France, warm within his shop, making violins and repairing instruments."

"Is that really a Romani folktale?" asked Mila.

"Of course, it is. It's not an old story. It's relatively new, but I'm of Romani heritage and I'm a folk that tells stories...So, it is a Romani folktale."

"Why did you tell me that story?"

"Child, I see you are searching. For some reason, you believe your searching must exclude your past, that your dream must be totally new and when you find that new breath of life it should be as if God touched you on the shoulder and you will become righteous, full of wonder and things will be perfect. Things are not perfect. Child, don't turn your back on who you are but use your roots to grow with. Everything that grows must have roots."

"How do you know this about me?"

"Now, I am an old traveler woman. You see my father was Romani, an ancient people, and my mother a modern French woman. With my old and new blood, I have an insight that is strong and an understanding that has grace. I see your story in your eyes, I can hear your story in your voice, and I can feel your story in your actions."

"I agree you are a wise woman and the story that you told I can identify with very much. But I must ask, with all your insight and understanding, why do you sit here under a bridge making bread on a stick?"

"My gift and dreams are to help and nourish the poor, tell stories to the people that need them and be kind to the fearful," she answered. "I learned this from my husband, Vano. Come help me make some bread on a stick. Put your hands into the dough. Working the dough will help you blend the old with the new."

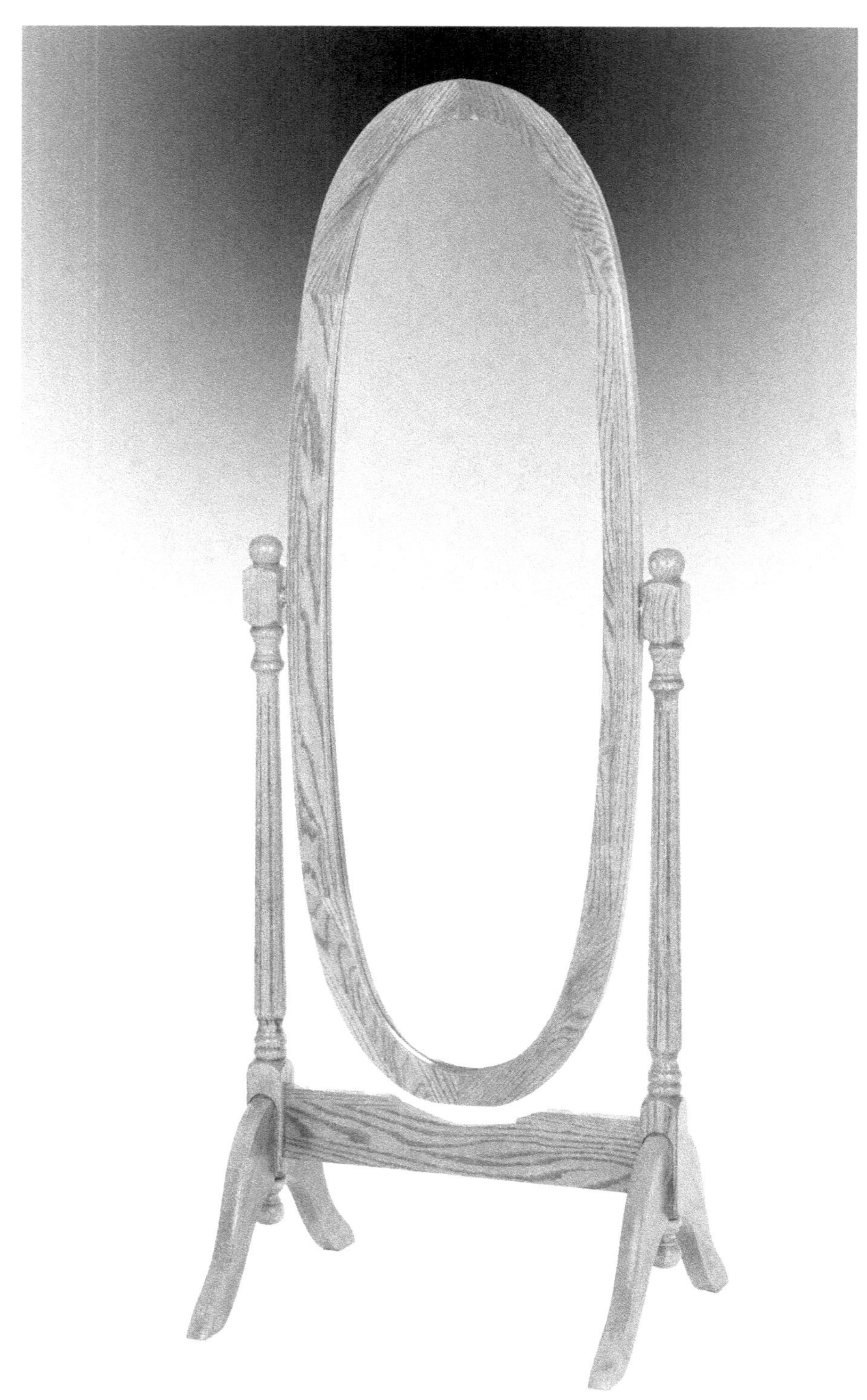

The Vanity Demon

The young Cassie sat at her vanity like a queen gazing into the mirror. Brushing her long, shiny black hair and staring at her beauty, she became fixated upon her eyes. There was oddness, maybe an evil childlike vanity in the stare, a strange look within a look. The young girl smiled with great pleasure as she went on brushing her hair.

As Cassie grew older, she spent more and more time sitting at her vanity, staring in the mirror and admiring her beauty. Sometimes her mother could hear her talking as if she was having a conversation, but when her mother opened the door, Cassie was sitting at the mirror brushing her hair.

She started to talk about a boy named Elliot and her mother asked if he was a boy from school.

"No," said Cassie.

"Well, how do you know him?"

"He comes from inside the looking glass."

"The looking glass?" said Mother. "Just what do you mean, 'the looking glass'?"

"He comes to visit me. He is very smart and knows most everything. And he is very handsome. He has dark hair like me and dark eyes like me and one dimple just like me, but on the right cheek not the left."

"What an imagination you have," said Mother. "Next time you see Elliot, tell him I said hello."

"I will, Mother."

Her mother ignored the imaginary friend most of the time, and Cassie learned to keep Elliot out of the conversation. When she was about fourteen, Mother saw that the door to Cassie's room was locked most of the time.

Mother would knock on the door and shout, "What are you doing in there?"

"Nothing," was always the answer.

Mother became less approving of this, and one day she peeked through the keyhole and saw Cassie dancing. Her arms were in a position as if she was holding someone, and her body seemed to be held as well.

"Cassie, what are you doing in there?"

"Nothing," said Cassie.

Mother unlocked the door and barged in, asking with whom she was dancing. At first, Cassie replied, "no one."

Mother pursued her questioning. When Cassie told her it was Elliot, mother just sat on the bed and shook her head as if to say no this can't be true. Then, Mother sprang up from the bed in fury.

"This is the end of this," said Mother. "I will not have my daughter dancing with some imaginary boy and spending hours looking into the mirror. There is no need for this nonsense."

Mother took the vanity mirror out of Cassie's room, and she didn't stop there. She even took the mirror on the closet door and the one in the downstairs hall. When Mother then realized that Cassie was spending more time in the bathroom, she confiscated every single mirror in the entire house and locked them in the attic.

Years passed and Cassie grew into a most beautiful young woman. Cassie, even though she was popular, kept people at a distance. Many of her friends thought her to be vain and envious. When she was out and about, she always looked for somewhere to see her reflection. It could be a storefront window, the chrome on an automobile, but the best was a public mirror.

She always was taking a glance at herself and when the time was right she would stand and gaze at her beauty ...She also was looking for Elliot. He only came into view when it was secure and others could not see him. Sometimes and only sometimes, when she passed by a storefront window she would catch a glimpse of Elliot waving at her. When she did a double take and looked again, he was gone, as if he was teasing her.

Cassie missed Elliot. She longed to gaze into his dark, knowing eyes and hear his voice that sounds how coffee with cream and sugar tastes. She even missed his touch, although it was smooth and cold.

Mirrors were slowly brought back into the house and Cassie seemed to act typical and responsible in front of them. Mother thought by now that she was over her vanity and that her imaginary friend was long forgotten. On her twentieth birthday, Mother surprised her with a beautiful full-length mirror. The mirror was a large beveled glass oval, freestanding, with two very nicely carved oak posts that supported it.

"Oh thank you, Mother!"

Cassie put her arms around her mother and gave her a big hug and a kiss. Although there was not a word about trust, growing out of childhood dreams, or even vainness. It was all asked by mother's eyes and answered with a nod and a smile from Cassie.

Cassie was much happier now that she had her looking glass back. She was always smiling, had more bounce in her step and seemed to be even more beautiful.

Elliot's presence was always in the mirror. He stayed the same age as Cassie and his handsomeness matched her beauty. His wit and charm were more advanced, leaving Cassie feeling somewhat naïve. Elliot came every night and they would have long, quiet conversation. He would step out of the looking glass. Making believe that they were at some elegant ball, they danced slow and romantic. As they danced, Elliot would whisper stories of traveling the world, being with the rich and famous, and how elegant and beautiful they both were. When Cassie looked into Elliot's eyes, it seemed as if she was looking into her own. It was an extraordinarily strange union. When they kissed, a bizarre longing intensified. Elliot always spent the night with her, but in the morning he was back in the mirror.

One day, Mother went into Cassie's room to borrow some lipstick. She had a feeling that she was not alone. She had an odd sensation that she was being watched. She became drawn to the large, freestanding mirror and when she walked toward it there was a flash within. She noticed a piece of paper stuck between the glass and the frame. It was a note with the writing facing the glass of the mirror.

Cassie's mother pulled it from the mirror and it read, "I'll be back after shopping."

There was a lipstick imprint, which matched a shade Cassie commonly wore, the same Mother had wished to borrow.

Mother walked out of the room quivering.

"I knew something was wrong," she shouted. "I just knew it. I don't know what I'm going to do with that girl."

When Cassie came home from shopping, she had a big smile on her face and her eyes were bright and cheerful.

"Oh, Mother, come upstairs and see the lovely dress I bought," said Cassie. "It was such a bargain. Can't believe I got it so cheap! Come, come on, Mother."

Cassie pulled her mother into her bedroom and dropped her packages on the bed. Out of the box came a red dress with a black satin collar. Cassie held it up, repeating how beautiful it was. She twirled around and then stood in front of the full length mirror gazing at herself.

"Isn't it great? Don't you just love it?" said Cassie.

"Yes," said Mother. "It is very lovely."

Mother sat on the bed watching Cassie twirling in front of the mirror. Her talk was exciting, all about how grand she looked and how jealous every girl would be. Cassie's mother sighed.

What should I say to Cassie? she thought. How can I tell her what I feel? How can I tell her what I fear? How can I ask her why this is happening?

She sighed again and shook her head as if to shake loose the sore, hurtful thoughts.

Mother rose from the bed and walked to her daughter and stood behind her, putting her hands on Cassie's shoulders. She drew her head to the side so that both were looking into the large oval mirror.

"Yes. You are beautiful," Mother said. "Almost too beautiful. You mustn't let your beauty take you away. Just look at yourself. I mean really look at you. Now tell me, what do you see?"

Cassie tried to turn and walk away but her mother gripped her shoulders harder.

"Mother, this is ridiculous!"

"No," said Mother. "Look at yourself. Tell me what you see."

Cassie stood with her eyes cast down. Then, she raised them and looked deep into the mirror. "It's beauty."

With a smile that suggested pleasure and in a tone that indicated immortality, she repeated,

"I see beauty. Lovely, elegant beauty. I see all the other women envying me. I see me...true beauty."

"Oh my dear," said Mother. "Life is not just about beauty. It is beyond beauty. You need to look within you and beyond the mirror. And what about this?"

Mother pulled the note from her pocket. Cassie laughed it off, saying it didn't mean anything. She really didn't know why she did it. It was a fun, stupid thing to do.

Mother said, "I don't believe you. You are hiding something. I don't understand why a daughter would lie to her mother the way you do. Do you still have that imaginary friend?"

Cassie could see her mother's hurt, anger and the embarrassment. She knew she could never tell her about Elliot. Cassie dropped her head and raised her eyes.

"No, not anymore."

Things started to change. Cassie became a more dutiful daughter, spent less time in her room and even got a job. She began working in a dress shop as a salesperson. It was the perfect job for her, telling women how lovely and pretty they looked. Her employer and customers loved her. She knew just how to stroke their vanity.

As time went on she acquired somewhat of a boyfriend, Benjamin J. Buckley, a fine, handsome young man who worked at the First National

Bank. He was a hard worker, smart, charming and was in love. It was Saturday date night when Ben was driving Cassie home from the movies and he told her about the promotion he was getting at the bank.

"This is a big step," said Ben. "I mean this is a big promotion, more responsibility, a lot more money, my own office and secretary."

"Oh, that's wonderful," said Cassie. "I'm very happy for you."

Ben started to hint about commitment and that they had been dating for four months and that they seemed happy. When Ben took Cassie's hand, thoughts flooded Cassie's mind. Fear started to bubble up, confusion brewed into panic, and Cassie had the urge to pull her hand away.

Thoughts of Elliot were attached to every emotion. The voice in Cassie's head reverberated with anxiety.

"Why can't things just stay the way they are? It is just fine working at the dress shop, seeing Ben once or twice a week, Mother is happy, and I can spend my nights with Elliot."

When the car came to a stop in front of Cassie's house, Ben turned to Cassie.

"I know that we've only been seeing each other for about four months but you hardly even let me kiss you," said Ben. "I want to be more than just a date. I think I've fallen in love with you."

Thoughts of Elliot emerged again.

"Oh Ben," Cassie said, "we need to take things slow, don't you think?"

She opened her purse and took out a small hand mirror. While looking into it, she said, "I'm afraid of commitment."

Ben pulled back and leaned against the car door. "There you go looking in the mirror again. It's as if you need a quick peek of vanity, like a smoker needs a quick puff on a cigarette or an alcoholic needs a quick drink. You need a quick look at yourself. Cassie, you are the most beautiful woman I've ever seen but I know there is more to you than just beauty. Let me in so I can show you that part of you...Please."

Cassie leaned over and kissed Ben, saying, "I must go now it's getting late. Things will be fine, just fine."

Cassie ran up to her room and sat in front of her vanity mirror. She started to brush her hair and stare into her eyes, when she heard Elliot's voice from behind her. She turned and saw Elliot stepping out of the full-length mirror.

"So, you have a boyfriend that wants more than holding hands and a kiss on the cheek," said Elliot. "Oh, yes I can tell. By the look on your face, and the racing of your heart beat."

Elliot's voice was different. He turned around, looking into the mirror, his back to Cassie.

"Tell me more about this young man. He is probably some store clerk that likes fishing, war movies and collects baseball cards. Or maybe he's a businessman that has a diamond pinky ring, smokes cigars and sucks his teeth. Does he dance stiff and jerky or fast and carefree? Is he as handsome as me?"

The tone of Elliot's voice was no longer coffee-like. It was sharp and stung like a poison dart with the venom oozing into her veins.

"He's a banker and a very good one. He doesn't collect baseball cards, smoke cigars, or suck his teeth. He dances divinely and he is handsome. But not as handsome as you...Oh Elliot, it just makes life easier if I have a steady date. I don't get all the questions or people trying to introduce me to somebody. It's convenient."

"It is so convenient that he falls in love with you and life is no longer easier, it becomes complicated."

Elliot turned around, his dark eyes disappearing into green pools of anger. He stared at Cassie. "Love is complicated but our love must remain simple. Just you and I and our beauty make three. You must end it with your banker friend Ben."

"How did you know his name?"

"I know many things," said Elliot.

He took her in his arms and kissed her.

"And you know it is necessary to end it," Elliot whispered.

Cassie didn't hear from Ben until Wednesday. He surprised her by asking if she was free, that he had something special to show her. Cassie said okay and found herself in Ben's car heading north and going out of town. They pulled off the main road and went down a gravel lane.

"Where are we going, Ben?"

"Don't worry. I'm sure you'll like it,"

They went around a bend and there stood a huge stone barn.

"Isn't she a beauty? Built about 1850. I inherited it from my grandfather, Willard Buckley, five years ago. It's my dream home now. Come inside, I can't wait to show you."

As the two entered and climbed the stairs to the second floor, Ben explained how the windows on the south side helped the heat and lighting. The appliances weren't installed yet in the kitchen, and when Cassie turned the knobs, no water came from the faucet. But she could see herself in the shiny chrome.

Ben then talked about the way he designed the open concept of the second and third floors. When they got to the third floor and looked into the openness, the beauty of the architecture all came together.

"This is simply marvelous," said Cassie. "I had no idea that you could do something like this. Ben, this is beautiful, truly beautiful."

"I'm glad you like it, said Ben. "It's been taking me more than four years to get this far."

Cassie leaned. The banister jiggled.

"Be careful," he said. "It's temporary."

They stood by the railing peering down as Ben explained his workmanship, Cassie spied a mirror.

Instantly, she said, "Ben, what is that?"

"Oh, that's an antique hall tree," said Ben. "Come and look. I knew you would like it. It's all oak. You have this big nice beveled mirror in the center, three double hooks on each side for hats or scarves, and a bench you can sit on and store things in."

Cassie ran her fingertips across the smooth woodgrain.

"Exquisite," slid out of her mouth.

She stood in front of the mirror, staring into it.

"Beautiful," she said.

Ben took her by the hand, ushering her back to the railing. Cassie turned to look back to get one more glimpse of herself when she saw Elliot stepping out of the mirror.

"Elliot!" She cried.

Elliot's eyes were burning with white heat as he rushed toward Ben.

"I told you that this must end," he said. "Now, it will."

"No, Elliot!" Cassie screamed.

Elliot slammed into Ben and over the railing they went. Down onto the floor with a smashing crash. Cassie stood, hands covering her eyes, screaming from behind her tears. She found the courage to inch her way to the edge. Peering over, she saw Ben's broken body face down and shattered mirror glass all around him.

There was no Elliot, just a broken mirror.

Cassie walked painfully to the hall tree and stared into the mirror watching her tears trickling across her cheeks.

"Beautiful?"

Very carefully, Cassie sat on the bench. Her arms stretched out, hands grasping the arms of the antique hall tree, looking like the constellation Queen Cassiopeia placed in the heavens tied to her throne.

The Power to Destroy

Ross pulls up in front of Paul's house. Paul gets in the car. Within less than a minute he goes into a story.

"I'm telling you, Ross, that I had the strangest dream. Did you ever have a dream that was so crystal clear, it seemed that it was real? And when you woke up, you thought maybe it could have been an out-of-body experience or something supernatural?"

"Yes," Ross confesses. "I had a few dreams that made me wonder if it was real or not."

Paul continues.

"So, in the dream, I'm hiking along this trail that is winding in and out of trees and rocks, similar to a trail at Hawk Mountain, that hugs along the edge of a sloping drop off. I go out to the edge to look at the view. I'm much higher than I thought and the drop is much steeper. But the view is spectacular, like a western landscape. Something catches my eye on the ground and when I stare at the rocks, I see two stag beetles. Two beetles that appear to be engaged in a battle. Do you know stag beetles?"

"No. I don't think I ever met any."

"They're amazing bugs. About an inch and a half to two inches long, a dark shiny brown or reddish brown and have enormous prehistoric-look-ing pinchers. The males have bigger pinchers that they use to fight with other males. The winner of the contest gets the right to court the female beetle. You know like deer or elk do. Thus, the name stag beetle"

Ross squints his eyes and asks, "How do you know all this?"

"Long story, but in the 70s I had them in my yard. I caught one and put it in a jar and took it to the County Farm Bureau. This geeky bug guy told me all about the stag beetle. He even asked if he could keep my specimen for his collection. I sold it to him for five bucks."

Ross turns his head.

"You're full of shit."

"No, I didn't sell it to him," Paul says. "But the rest is true. Anyway, stag beetles live in the ground or in old decaying wood or roots. And they only come out at night. So here are two stag beetles in combat on dry rocky ground in the middle of a bright sunny day. I look at them for a while. Then, I have the impulse to kick them off the edge, so they can have an aerial battle."

Ross laughs.

"You're sick," he says.

"Now listen. I don't kick them off the cliff because something tells me, 'I don't have the right to do that.' So, I continue on my hike with a feeling of doing the right thing. On the way back, I stop to see if the stag beetles are still there and they were. They're looking even more magnificent with their deep brown shells shining in the sunlight. Then I say aloud, 'Only God has the right to destroy.'"

"Very strange dream. How can you remember all that and in so much detail?"

"Well, when I wake up I write down my dreams."

"You really write your dreams down?"

"I do. It's fun."

Paul and Ross have been friends for twenty-two years. They met at McQuaid's Tavern in their late twenties, when they both played on McQuaid's softball team.

Paul is an antique and vintage collectibles dealer who sells at shows and flea markets. He also has a booth in an antique and collectibles co-op in Bucks County. Ross works at the post office as a letter carrier in Doylestown. Ross is more athletic and sports minded. He stands 6-foot, medium build, thick wavy reddish-brown hair, and sports a Mike Schmidt mustache. Paul's an inch or two shorter than Ross, also medium build, and has brown thinning hair graying at the temples. Paul is more inquisitive and reads informational periodicals.

Ross pulls the car off the road onto the gravel parking area.

"Okay, Paul, we're here It's just a short 10 to 15-minute walk but it's uphill," Ross warns. "The view is worth it."

"I've never been to this part of Bucks County," says Paul.

"It's really nice around here," Ross says. "Afterwards, we'll stop in town to get ice cream or something to eat."

After the short walk, Paul stands by an old stone wall looking out over the valley. "This is really a beautiful spot. It captures the essence of Bucks County."

Ross nods.

"A lot of people come here to take pictures and I've been here before when artists have their easels set up and they're painting the beauty of the land. It was a treat to watch them."

"This is magnificent, Ross. Look how the wooded area sweeps down to the back of the farmhouse. The front of the farmhouse is staring out to the open fields that change from season to season and year to year. The big oak tree next to the farmhouse stands like a sentry, a gatekeeper that allows the people to pass through the gate on their way to the Enchanted Forest."

"Most people see the simplicity of beauty, but you always see a story."

"Oh, speaking of stories, let me tell you the rest of the dream."

"There's more? Like I'm surprised."

Paul ignores Ross.

"Now, this is the good part. Remember, I stopped and saw the stag beetles again and I said out loud, 'Only God has the right to destroy.' So, after my hike, I'm driving home and listening to an old-time radio show. Kind of a mystery, detective story, like Mike Hammer."

"This is still part of the dream?" Ross asks.

Yes. In my dream, I'm driving and listening to the radio. So, in the radio show, this police lieutenant, Lieutenant Patterson, is telling another cop my story."

"This is all part of the dream? So, what do you mean, 'your story'?"

"Listen, he's telling the other cop about an incident that happened with a detective partner by the name Duffy. He and Duffy and two other uniformed cops are on a stakeout. The younger uniformed cop sees two stag beetles on the ground engaged in their battle. The young cop says, 'Look at the two bugs going at it.' He raises his foot to smash them. Duffy grabs his arm and pulls him back and says, 'Only God has the right or the power to destroy.' Then Lieutenant Patterson says to the young police offi-cer, 'Every time before I fire my gun, I think that, "Only God has the right or the power to destroy."' Then I woke up. Pretty weird?"

"Yeah, that is pretty weird. As well as strange, bizarre, freaky, and freakin' creepy...like you. A dream that has stories within stories. Let me see if I got all of this straight. You are having a dream, and in the dream you are taking a hike and see two stag beetles. And you say, 'only God has the right or the power to destroy.' Then you're driving a car, still in the dream, and you listen to a radio show, where some Lieutenant tells a story about this dude named Duffy. And Duffy pulls this cop away from step-ping on two stag beetles, and says, 'Only God has the right or the power to destroy.' Then the Lieutenant cop says, 'Before I fire my gun I think about what Duffy said about only God having the right or the power to destroy.'"

"Yes, you got it. I'm impressed, your attention span is much better than I thought. But you have to admit it was an interesting dream."

They smile and nod at each other.

"It is interesting and freaking weird," Ross says. "Now, let me take you to an interesting place to have ice cream"

A few minutes later, they pull into another parking lot and park facing the building. The big green sign on the porch roof in white lettering, reads:

"Greenawalt's Dairy

The best ice cream and dairy products in the county"

Paul asks if the sign is true.

"Let's find out for ourselves," Ross says.

They step up on the long wrap-around porch filled with people licking ice cream cones, sitting in rocking chairs and on long green benches. Ross pulls open the old, wooden frame screen door, which of course is painted in green. Printed in the middle of the top screen is the dairy's logo. Everything inside is sparkling in green, white or chrome.

"I think we just stepped into the 1950s," Paul says.

"Isn't this neat? I love the old soda fountain counter with the stools that have seats that spin around on top of the chrome pedestals." Ross smiles a boastful smile. "When I was a kid, my dad would bring me here. I would sit on the stool and spin around as I ate my ice cream."

"A little flash of the past for you," Paul says kindly.

As they stand in line and marvel at the old advertisement signs of the past, the screen door swings open and slams shut with a bang. A man shouts, but it's hard to make sense of his words. Paul and Ross turn toward the commotion and see a curly headed man in his mid-twenties with tattooed arms and a tank top, screaming at a young blond woman in a booth.

"You destroyed my life," he screams, slapping his hand hard on the table. "You dirty bitch! You destroyed my life."

The young woman at first was startled and cringed in the corner of the booth. She soon gathers some courage and slides to the end of the booth. Standing up with defiance, she shakes her ice cream cone and points it at the screaming man like a mother or a teacher reprimanding a child. The man raises his arms alongside his head. He shakes his hands back and forth.

"You destroyed my life," he continues to scream.

She, still pointing her ice cream cone, steps forward and the man steps back. Now, pointing the ice cream cone directly in his face, almost touching his nose, she says loud and without any fear, "Only God has the power and the right to destroy."

The man stops screaming and takes another step backward. He hesitates.

"You did destroy my life," he stutters out, slowly, and not as loud. "You took everything from me."

The young woman pushes back her long blond hair, and in a lower voice repeats, "Only God has the power and the right to destroy."

His tattooed arms drop to his side. He looks at the floor and then slowly brings his head up. "But I'm broken, miserable, and lost," he says. "I'm living in a state of chaos. I'm destroyed."

"No, you're not," she says in a firm voice. "Lost, but not destroyed."

The young woman's thin body becomes relaxed. In a kinder voice, she says, "My ice cream is melting. Do you want a lick?"

The curly headed man's anger deflates.

"You know I don't like strawberry."

"But it's dripping on my hand," she says. "Go ahead, taste a little bit of something that you don't like."

He pulls her hand close to him and takes two licks of the ice cream cone.

"Not too bad," he admits.

The woman smiles.

"We can sure fuck things up," she says, "but only God has the power and the right to destroy."

The couple walk out of the ice cream parlor. The screen door slams behind them.

"Wow, that was amazing," Paul says.

"Yes it was," Ross agrees. "Real life drama at Greenawalt's. She reminds me of a woman I went out with. Could have been her sister. She wasn't as pretty as her, but she was as feisty as her. Do you think we can destroy some ice cream?"

Angel in the Pines

It's the second day of 2018. I'm sitting in City Diner at Broad and South, sipping coffee, as memories from thirty years ago swirl and swell in my mind. A young guy in his thirties comes in and sits two stools from me. As he takes off his gloves and shoves them into his coat pocket, he nods to the waitress.

"Good morning, Liz."

She smiles at him.

"Happy New Year, Bill. Two eggs over easy, rye toast and coffee?"

"Yeah, that's good. Oh, and Happy New Year to you. Did you work yesterday? Must've been pretty crazy. With it being so cold and all."

Liz sets coffee in front of the guy. She nods her head and rolls her eyes.

"Constant flow of people. The line was down the street and the owner had to stand by the door and let people in while other people were leaving. But no mishaps with drunks, drugs, or anything out of the ordinary from the New Year's Day crowd."

"I guess you made some money though?"

"Yes." She smiled. "Long hours and hard work. But when you're busy time goes fast. I'm dead on my feet today, but it was worth it."

The young fellow reaches to the other end of the counter and with his fingertips, grabs the newspaper and slides it to him. He glances over at me.

"Happy New Year."

"Yeah, Happy New Year," I say.

"Some parade. I watched parts of it on TV. They say it was the third coldest New Year's day parade in history . It was only 11°. You wouldn't catch me standing on the sidewalk watching guys strutting down the street in feathers playing old-time music. Way too cold for that."

I glance out the window and see debris on the empty street. I look back at the young guy.

"Some parade, but now it looks like a ghost town," I say. "At one time I was part of Philadelphia's finest tradition. I was a mummer for over fifteen years. I started out playing the banjo with the Walking Aces when I was nineteen years old. I didn't even know how to play the banjo, I just wanted to be a mummer. I paraded in all kinds of weather, and when it's cold, it's harder on the spectator than the mummer. We're moving and playing while the spectators must stand around."

The young guy looks at me with a blank face.

"I moved up the ranks fast and became one of the youngest captains of a string band. Yeah, the Walking Aces was a good club, but that's all gone. They broke up thirty years ago in '88."

He raises his eyebrows. "You were the captain? The guy out in front of the string band with all the plumage struttin' his stuff?"

"Yeah, that was me."

"What happened?"

"What do ya mean what happened?"

"I mean, why did you stop being a mummer? And why did the club break up?"

I stare out the window. After collecting my thoughts, I turn and look this young man in the eye and I had this incredible urge to finally tell it all.

And without taking one second to think, my secret, my incredible secret, starts to flow from my lips. I point out the window.

"It happened right out there on Broad Street, Broad and South. Thirty years ago, New Year's Day, 1988."

I pause for a moment and my emotions build inside me. I'm surprised I'm doing this. Even though my fear is damming up the story that I so long to tell, I go on.

I clear my throat and stutter…"It was, it was, right out there when the wind came. I was in front strutting to Golden Slippers. My back plumage was magnificent, over 200 ostrich feathers. With it on my shoulders we reached to nine feet high and the weight was 55 pounds with my head-dress. The weather was perfect for a parade, the high that day was something like 44° and just a slight little breeze. Then from behind me, I heard the music become jumbled and out of tune. The crowd was murmuring and there were shrieks of…"Oh, my God." Papers, feathers, and sheet music flew by me. I started to turn to see what was happening behind me, when a rush of wind echoed in my ears. I started being pushed from behind, a force that I could not stop. Then the sensation of being lifted into the air. The more I fought the force from behind, the higher I seemed to go. I glanced down, I must've been fifteen or twenty feet above the street. The wind pulled my guide lines and my feet were kicking in the air. I was lifted higher and higher and higher all the while moving forward, almost straight up. I got up so high that I naturally stopped fighting for fear that I would fall and crash to the ground.

"You mean you were actually floating in the air?"

"It was more like drifting or sailing."

"This is incredible. How high were you?"

"Pretty goddamn high. I glided with the wind at my back, so I was moving north on Broad Street. I was as high as Billy Penn. I looked at his face and he seemed surprised to see me. I'm suspended between William Penn on top of City Hall and the new building. You know, the first building that was taller than him."

"You mean One Liberty Plaza?"

"Yeah, I guess that's the name. I caught a thermal, just like the birds of prey do. In a slow lazy circle, I flew higher and higher and higher. My heart was pounding, and I was chanting in time with my heartbeat, God please help me. God please help me."

The young guy looks at the waitress and then to me.

"This is more than incredible. It's freaking nuts."

He points to his ear with his index finger and makes a circular motion.

"I know it sounds crazy," I admit. "That's why I haven't told the story in thirty years."

Liz puts her hands on the counter and leans a bit forward.

"Go on," she prods me. "Tell the story. Don't let us hang here in midair."

"From the ground I must've been out of sight. Suddenly, I started to drop like a skydiver, and a scream came out of me that the heavens could hear. I was soaring on an angle headed toward the Delaware River. It must've been instinct that I positioned my body in such a manner that allowed the sky to sail over me. I felt like a superhero—Superman, Batman, and the Flash, all rolled into one. From Camden, I sailed over New Jersey in a straight line to the Pine Barrens where I was dropped in the middle of nowhere, my plumage and me stuck on a pine tree."

Liz slaps her hand on the counter and points her finger at me.

"Wait a minute! Wait a minute!" she interrupts. "I remember hearing something about this. Some mummer flew up in the air and disappeared."

She pulls her phone from her apron pocket and pokes it with her finger. She then progresses from finger-poking to thumb-bashing. The young fellow does the same with his phone. The conversation between them passes in fragments and groups of letters, a language I don't understand. Yo, what the fuck are they talking about, I ask myself.

The young fella suddenly shouts.

"I got it, I got it! Look at the *Philadelphia Inquirer* archives, January 1, 2008. There's an article by Tom Rittenhouse."

"Okay," says Liz. "It reads, 'The Disappearing Mummer...The Captain of the Walking Aces, Vincent De Christopher, known to his fellow mummers as Vinny De, disappeared twenty years ago as he sailed down Broad Street and into the heavens. It was the biggest Philadelphia mystery in the twentieth century and remains a mystery to this day. Where did Vinny De go?'"

Liz stops reading the article then looks at me.

"He didn't go anywheres," she says with a laugh. "He's sittin' right here."

Both stare at me and just about in unison say, "Is that true? Are you really Vinny De?"

I nod. With a bittersweet urgency, I continue to tell the story.

"If you read the papers from that time to now, you will find 100 different theories and beliefs of what happened. Mostly all think it's a hoax. The most popular belief is that a helicopter high in the sky or somehow undetected was the cause of the wind that blew down Broad Street and the means that pulled me off the street. Somehow an invisible cable attached to the helicopter drew me into the heavens. Others thought it was a dummy. Some even claimed it was a helium balloon made to look like me that drifted into the sky. One story connected me to the Philly mob and claimed I was rubbed out. Aliens sucked me up into some spaceship. Some said I was the start of the curse of Billy Penn, you know One Liberty Place was the first building taller than Billy Penn. There was a gentlemen's agreement that became a tradition, that no building in Philadelphia could be taller than the statue of William Penn on City Hall. It became a curse and no Philadelphia sports team could win a championship. Very few could see the truth. I was taken away by some cursed force."

The young man leans closer to me with a face full of doubt. "You mean, you get blown down the street and float up into the air, drift across New Jersey, and drop into the Pine Barrens and nobody knows where the hell you are for thirty years? If you are the disappearing Vinny De, you need to come up with a better story than 'some cursed force.'"

"Young man, what is your name?" I ask.

"Bill," he answers.

"Okay, Bill. If you have some time, I'll tell you the whole story. But you can't interrupt. You gotta sit and listen."

"Yeah, okay. I can listen."

I sip some coffee, clear my throat and ask Liz for a glass of water. In a blink of an eye, the water appears in front of me. I thank her and take a sip. With nervousness, I start my story.

"When I was soaring, gliding, flying—whatever it was—it didn't seem real. I was cold, the wind rushed across my face and I was numb with fear.

Time was not part of it. I couldn't tell you if it took hours or minutes to reach the Pine Barrens. I know I'll never forget it, even though it was like a dream. Some magical understanding came to me without me knowing how or why. It was just there inside me."

Bill leans forward as if he wants to ask a question. I put my hand up and shake my head no. He sits back on his stool and Liz stands with her arms folded across her chest.

"I come down with a crash and a jerk. I'm hung up on a pine tree. I'm hanging there. You know suspended like some paratrooper from a World War II movie. My plumage from the back costume was stuck, and I mean stuck! No matter what or how I wiggled or squirmed. And I tried to rip away my cords. I even tried to jump, which was totally useless. There I was like a marionette hanging from strings. I called out for help. Nothing happened. I screamed out, even though I knew it was useless. I started with a goddamn it which led to questioning God. By late afternoon, when the sun was going down and the coldness was creeping into my bones, the real prayers, I mean real prayers with tears of fear were spoken into the wilderness."

I pause for some water. Bill and Liz stare at me in silence, a silence begging to ask questions.

"Then the most terrifying, horrible thing that you could imagine happened. I'm hanging there, praying with all my heart, asking God for help. The sky glows a pinkish orange-red and the pine trees fade into darkness. I hear a scream...a bloodcurdling scream, a sound like I never heard before. I hang motionless."

I move toward them a little for emphasis.

"Again this scream comes from the pine trees. I imagine that only a mountain lion could make a scream like that. Twigs snap. Branches rustle. Then the scream once more...but closer. Silence...then like a shot from a cannon the loudest scream yet. It echoes in the woods and my spine tingles. I tried to scream back, but not a sound came out. I see two red glowing spots and a silhouette of huge bat wings. The screaming mountain lion vanishes from my thoughts. I close my eyes and pray. When I open them, a horse face with red eyes and two bony horns above the ears is... somehow...like three feet away from me. It pokes its nose a little closer and sniffs. I scream, and I can scream now, the loudest and the most fearful scream I ever made. The monster jumps back and roars his scream right in my face...I guess I passed out."

I pause for some coffee. Memories, thoughts and emotions bounce inside me. But one thing came back strong, stronger than all the other memories. It almost made me choke on my coffee. The smell. I could smell the smell. Like a musty, old blanket, strong ammonia yet putridly sweet. I wanted to light a cigarette just to rid myself of it.

Bill opens his mouth and as a sound comes out, I wave my hand 'no.'

"Look, I never really told this story to anyone. I've relived it many times, but I never spoke of it." I continue. "So, I'm passed out. I don't know how long I was out, could've been hours, days or even longer. But when I come to, I am in some kind of nest. My ostrich plumes are underneath me and a dirty blanket on top. It's cold. You know, it is freaking January and I'm lying on dried ferns and straw with my ostrich plumes. I'm in this, like, gorge with pine branches that makes a wigwam thing. It's hard to explain, the ground is dug out about 3-foot-deep and maybe 15-foot-wide. Around it, there's a structure of pine branches that creates a shelter like a beavers lodge…And it's quiet. You know that quiet when snow is falling? That type of quiet. Then the smell hits me. A horrible, musty, rotten egg, low-tide rankness, a decaying stench that hits your nostrils making you gag and cough."

I gaze at Liz and ask for another cup of coffee. She nods 'yes.'

"I think the aroma of fresh brewed coffee can't hurt right about now," she says.

She's right. She places a fresh cup of coffee in front of me and, after a few sips, I start again.

"I stand and look around this strange hut. Rustling branches break the silence and the red eyes peer at me from outside the shelter. The monster's head pushes inside and sniffs. I'm frozen with panic. I mean, I wanna run or scream, but I just stand there. I tell myself, I don't fucking believe this is happening. Then the creature steps into the hut, sticking his nose inches from my face. I could feel his bristly whiskers tapping my cheek. In one quick move and a jerk, it grabbed me with its teeth, luckily by the back of my costume. Like a cat carries a kitten, I was taken outside and placed against the pine tree."

I drink some more coffee and stare at the counter for a moment and then continue with my story.

"I'm up against a tree and this creature is staring at me…and I at him, knowing I'm in deep shit. He was big, but not as big as I thought it was. Face like a horse, horns like a goat and a goatee. A kangaroo- or dinosaur-type shaped body, with small arms and no fingers, only talons. Strong ostrich legs with hooves and a serpent's tail, forked at the end. He used that tail like another arm. He had huge, bat-like wings."

Liz interrupts, blurting a question about the color of the monster.

"That's not a real question," she quickly adds. "I know we're supposed to just listen."

Bill leans forward pointing his finger.

"You're talking about the Jersey Devil," he says.

Liz covers her mouth.

"Oh, my God!" she gasps. "The Jersey Devil!"

I nod.

"Yes. The Jersey Devil," I confirm. "The devil is reddish, orangish, grayish, and sometimes a tinge of blue green—but mostly a reddish. It's hard to tell what color he is. Like so many things about him, it changes rapidly. Sometimes he seems quite large. Other times, he's not much bigger than me. I personally think he's a shapeshifter."

Just by the looks on their faces, I know Liz and especially Bill have 101 questions for me. Once again, I pause to sip some coffee and quickly explain my theory.

"I don't quite understand it myself. The Devil seems to live in a different time frame than we do. It doesn't seem like I was away for thirty years. I know I've been away for some time, but I couldn't tell you how long. When I was with the Devil, time seemed to move slow but also fast. There are so many paradoxes that it is impossible to comprehend. I just accepted it."

I give myself a moment.

"Look, I don't want to get ahead of myself," I say. "I was standing in front of the tree and the Devil was checking me out. Our first face-to-face. He continued sniffing me and he would touch me with his nose. His nose was soft and sensitive like a horse's, and gentle, very gentle...moving slow and sniffing all the time...as if he was taking in so much information, like a blind person reading Braille. I'm frozen with fear. I think, here is this terrifying monster with horns, claws, hoofs and a freakin' tail sniffing me...and touching me ever so gentle. Do you see the paradox? A frightening presence, but a nose full of grace. It seemed like forever. I'm deep in the woods being scrutinized by this monster. It's cold and dank and I'm dressed in silk and sequins with golden shoes. Scared shitless."

I pause to clear my throat. I take a drink of water. Liz tells the other waitress that she's on her break. Bill rearranges his body on his stool, sitting with his arms folded. The look on his face tells me he thinks I'm crazy, but he tells me to go on.

"Then, the most amazing thing happens. The Devil steps back and with his tail he clears an area in the sandy soil. His eyes are no longer red, but a soft yellow amber, like a cat's. With one point of his tail he draws a crude picture in the sand. He lifts his tails and points to me, and then he points to the picture in the sand. He does this a couple of times. Then he motions with his right claw-like hand for me to look at the drawing. He looks to the sky and then he points from me to the drawing. He does this several times. I finally look at the drawing. It was a crude and child-like drawing of me. He saw me fall from the sky. I nod, look into the eyes of the Devil, which are now changing to a yellowish-green, and my fear fades—but I still have terrifying visions of being torn apart and eaten. I don't know what to do. I'm standing there searching for some thought, some idea, but I keep thinking that I'm in the Twilight Zone."

"Star Wars," Bill chimes in. "You're in Star Wars communicating with an alien."

"Sure," I say. "Star Wars."

Bill and Liz laugh uneasily.

"A movie trilogy about Vinny De and the Jersey Devil," Liz ponders.

"No way," I answer. "At the time, I had no idea what to do, so I mimicked him. I clear away a spot, grab a stick, and draw a picture of us. I made me looking very scared. I point to the picture, and pantomime my fear. The demon relaxed and he nodded. We knew trust needed to be established. It was simple, and sometimes chaotic, but we had established our form of conversation. The more we communicated, the more we trusted. The more we trusted, the more we communicated. His innocence and his want to communicate with me seemed to cancel out my fear. The less I feared the Jersey Devil, the more my inner demons disappeared. Now, The Jersey Devil was like a mood ring. Do you remember mood rings from the seventies? They would change color by how much tension you were feeling."

Bill and Liz both nodded.

"So, the redder he was, the more angry or fearful he was. As his color changed from red to orange, to yellow, to green, and then to a bluish green, the less fearful and more trusting he became. He was less confused and more understanding, and when he became bluish green, the more gentle and kinder he became. I have to take a bathroom break. I'll be right back."

I don't know what Bill and Liz said to each other while I was gone, but I can imagine. I know what I would be thinking. This old guy is crazy. Floating in the sky. Having a conversation with the Jersey Devil. What a nut case. But, as soon as I get back, it's Bill who starts asking questions, his tone ripe with sarcasm.

"Why you? Why were you picked?" he says. "What makes you qualified to have a conversation with the Jersey Devil?"

I shrug.

"Just listen, will ya? You have to understand more about the Jersey Devil and then you'll know more about me. This is some heavy shit," I warn. "It was as if we were suspended in time. When we communicated, nothing else mattered. We were in the moment."

I pause.

"The main thing I learned is that The Jersey Devil is not the beast that people make him out to be. He was born human. He has the soul of an innocent child, that's why there's so much of a paradox with the Jersey Devil. His own mother cursed him and allowed Satan to transform him into a devil."

Liz looks tense.

"Listen, I need to do some work before I get my butt fired," she says, "but the breakfast crowd has thinned out...let me talk to Tony."

She walks into the kitchen.

"Tony's the boss," Bill explains.

Liz returns, taking off her waitress apron, and directs us to the booths. Bill picks one and slides in. I sit opposite him.

"Can I get you anything to eat?" Liz asks.

She's a waitress, I figure she's asking out of habit. But then she looks directly at me.

"Come on," she says. "What would you really like to eat? There's got to be something."

"How's your cheesesteaks?" I reply.

She smiles. "This is Philly. So they're pretty good. Sauce and onions? Fries, too?"

"Yeah, and maybe cheese fries and a Coke."

Bill orders a sticky bun and more coffee. Liz hustles away and comes back with the coffee pot, Bill's pastry and my Coke. She refills Bill's mug and puts the glass carafe on the table.

"There are some different stories about how he came to be. The main legend of The Jersey Devil starts with Mother Leeds," I explain. "The year is 1735. Mother Leeds had twelve children and her thirteenth pregnancy was extremely hard and the birth even harder. The pain of labor caused her to curse the child, swearing that it must be the devil. And so, within moments, the child transformed into this creature that we know as The Jersey Devil."

Liz retrieves her phone. Her fingers tap across the screen. "The Jersey Devil, I got it."

"Yeah, Wikipedia," Bill adds.

He looks at his phone. I stop telling my tale and watch them pushing buttons with their thumbs. They mutter as they research The Jersey Devil's folklore. A different waitress comes to the table and delivers my cheesesteak and fries. I thank her. I cut the steak in half and take a big bite. The juice and sauce run out of the corner of my mouth.

"Gooooood," I mumble through my full mouth.

While I eat, Liz and Bill discuss the legend of The Jersey Devil. And it seems that we've all come to the same understanding. But they soon turn to question my involvement in the story. Why me? Why am I a part of this crazy story? Why Vinny De Christopher? I set down my sandwich and wipe my mouth before answering.

"Look, I didn't get this right away," I say. "I was just trying to survive. This creature looks horrible, smells bad, and changes mood rapidly. I'm in constant fear. I mean, I could wake up and be his breakfast. But little by little, through the drawings, pointing, and pantomiming, I got the feeling that I was something special to him. I was some kind of angel. I descended from the sky with plumes, weaker and gentler, completely non-threatening, and for the first time in the creature's life, someone wanted to communicate with him. I mean nobody was shooting at him or trying to trap him. I didn't come roaring through the Pine Barrens on some loud ass four-wheeler. I'm guessing it was extremely difficult for him. I have the feeling that The Devil wanted me to end his curse."

"You mean like do something magical?" asks Liz.

Bill leans forward. He has a wide-eyed expression.

"Like kissing him on his soft and sensitive nose," he says.

"No. I don't mean that at all. He's not like a frog prince in a freakin' fairytale," I reply. "What I'm sayin' is that he wanted some help. He knew something was wrong."

I take a couple more bites of my cheesesteak and sip some Coke. I look at Liz and Bill. I knew I had to tell them about the real me.

"I wasn't such a nice guy. The truth is the Walking Aces were going to boot me out," I reveal. "The only reason I could be in the parade was the time factor. They could have replaced me, but nobody would've known the routine."

Before they could ask any questions, I continue.

"I was good at strutting and organizing the guys, but I was a real S.O.B. I was quick with my temper and I was a screamer, a bully, and a know-it-all," I explain. "I lived alone in this little house in South Philly, the house I grew up in. By the time I was twenty-four both of my parents were gone. When my folks died, being the only kid, I got the house. I worked at this shitty little pallet company, at a nowhere job, stapling wood pallets together. Had no wife or girlfriend. I was pretty much a loner. The only thing I did was be a mummer. I was pretty miserable."

"That doesn't sound that horrible," Bill says. "My life is pretty much like that now."

"I know it sounds like a bullshit problem. You know in the cartoons when you see the angel on one shoulder and the devil on the other and there is this conversation where the devil is tempting you while the angel's telling you to go on the straight and narrow path? Well I would spit at the devil and tell God to leave me alone. That left me with me. One day, I was doing the dishes and my mind started to whirl. Next thing you know, I flew into this rage, breaking dishes and throwing glasses, shouting fuck this and fuck that, screaming at God and cursing the devil. Then I say it loud and clear, I should be the devil. It was as if I cursed myself. I developed a miserable attitude and a chip on my shoulder. I loved to torment people. I had a meanness that gave me pleasure and an arrogance that hid the hatred I had for myself. I vandalized places that I liked, like the diner where I ate breakfast every morning and my neighbor's cars. I found myself pissing on my neighbor's petunias. I was telling the whole world to kiss my ass. This went on for about a year or so, until that wind came on New Year's Day and blew me to New Jersey."

We sit in silence, while I nibble at my fries. Liz puts her hand across the table to touch mine, but I yank my hand away.

"I'm not an angel. I'm no more an angel than the Jersey Devil himself, the poor soul," I say. "There were times I thought for hours about how to kill the beast or to trap him, at least slow him down so I could escape. But I was never a prisoner. I thought of myself as a prisoner. The truth is I did not have to scheme or trick him. I just walked away. I walked away as the Monster of the Pines stood there and released a hurtful moan of sadness and disappointment."

Bill puts down his coffee. "What do you mean you walked away?"

"I waved goodbye and I simply walked off."

"But where did you go?" Bill asks.

"Now that's a whole other story. I had no fucking idea where I was, so I just started walking," I explain. "You need to realize that, at first, I had no sense of time. I can't say to this day how long I was with him, but when I finally read a newspaper, it was June, 1992. How could it be nine-ty-two? Where did four years ago? When I left, I was still in my mummer's costume, all sparkly and shiny with golden shoes. Walking through the woods, I thought, what if somebody sees me dressed this way? They'll think I'm from outer space or some crazy cult. So, I came up with a story that is half true. I got so drunk at the Mummer's Day parade that I woke up here in the Pine Barrens and was trying to find my way out. I thought I was only gone a couple of weeks or so. I came to a road. It was a well-traveled, sandy dirt road. I had no idea which direction to take, so I went right. I walked for a long while, 'til I came to a blacktop road and a house. It seemed like nobody was home, but there was wash on the line—a pair of pants and a shirt that fit—which I stole. I went into the woods, put on my new clothes and buried my costume. I continued down the road 'til I came to a village, Chatsworth, and a small rustic inn. I went to the back door and acted like a homeless person, which I was, and asked for a handout. That handout turned into a job and that job got me a cabin to live in."

I pause for another bite and more Coke. Bill and Liz fire questions at me. I wave my hand.

"I know you want to know why didn't I go home. The truth of the matter is, what the fuck was I going to say? That I was lifted away by a magical freak force of nature? Sailed across New Jersey to the Pine Barrens and hung out with the Jersey Devil? That's crazy. True but freaking crazy. So, I just laid low and pondered what the hell really happened.

I read every newspaper I could and asked anybody and everybody about the Jersey Devil. Finally, I made my way to the library in Vincentown where I could research the 1988 Mummer's Parade and learn more about the Jersey Devil. This took about six months. From time to time, I would return to that sandy dirt road and go to the spot where I came out of the woods. I'd stand there, waiting.

Then one day, I heard the rustling in the pines and a scream came out of the forest. I saw a glimpse of him amongst the trees. He went back and forth like a flash. He walked out of the woods with his long neck stretched and his big nose sniffing. He stood in front of me, his color was changing to an orange yellowish green. I smiled and patted his nose. That was the very first time I touched him. We went into the pines and just sat with each other. Once again, a time lapse took place. When I got back to my cabin, it seemed like nobody had been there for a while and when I went to my job, my boss was furious with me. He screamed at me.

'Where the Hell were you? Months go by and you show up ready to work like nothing happened? We had the cops looking for you! I mean, what the fuck, it doesn't make any sense!'

Somehow, we worked it out. I worked in the summer when the restaurant was busy and took off with the Jersey Devil in the winter. I made my own hut, away from that Devil's smell and I brought things that I wanted or needed, like soap, water, personal things. I also brought books, storybooks with pictures. We would sit for hours, maybe days, and read picture books. He was like a child and wanted to read the same story over and over. He especially liked *Peter and the Dragon, Goldilocks and the Three Bears,* and *The Wild Thing.* I sat, in a folding chair I brought, and Jersey looked over my shoulder as I read out loud. I don't think he was too interested in the words, but he sure did like the pictures.

He taught me about nature. The first thing he taught me was to be still, to sit and watch and wait. If you are still enough, your five senses will receive things that you didn't even know were there. Before, I never got to see animals behaving as if no one was watching, but your five senses open avenues of perception and awareness. You become in tune with nature and can see the harmony and growth happening within the Pine Barrens. I started to pick up thoughts and feelings from Jersey himself, like a form of telepathy."

I pause for some more Coke and mention that I still can't get over not being able to smoke in restaurants. Liz suggests visiting the staff smoking area.

"Good idea," I say.

We stand. Bill brings his mug, having refilled it from the carafe Liz left on the table. Liz places the now empty carafe on the coffee machine as we head out the rear of the diner. There are a couple of old chairs and an ashtray off in the corner of the area where trucks pull in for delivery. We were out of the wind, so it wasn't too bad. Liz and I light up cigarettes. Bill puts his gloves back on and sips his coffee.

I tell them about the time I tried to teach Jersey how to smoke.

"The first time I lit a cigarette in front of Jersey, it scared the crap out of him. He jumped back, turning bright red, and glared at me. I continued to smoke as if nothing was wrong. He was very curious about the smoke coming out of my mouth. He sniffed the air, then tried to bite the smoke, and finally he waved it away with his tail. Little by little, he got used to me smoking, so one day I offered him a cigarette. I lit a cigarette and put it to his lips. He pulled back and his face became red."

"Danger," Bill interrupts.

"No shit, Sherlock. I lit another cigarette. He gets the idea that one is for me and the other is for him. I take a deep drag and blow the smoke from my nose. Now he's really interested. I get him to let me hold a cigarette to his lips, but his lips are too big and wet for him to keep it in his mouth. I guess he got the taste of it. I would do cigarette tricks. I'd stick the cigarette in one of my nostrils and inhale and blow smoke out of my mouth. I put a cigarette to my navel making believe I inhaled from there. Jersey was just like a kid and that was the first time I saw any part of humor in him. Eventually, I brought cigars and he could handle that, but most of the time he ate them."

Liz and Bill laugh.

"Things are going good for about eight years. But Jersey wasn't progressing like he had been. I might have been getting bored. Then the restaurant was sold so I had to find a new job. I worked a couple years with a landscaper and with a guy building decks. I didn't have a car. I had a bicycle, but that couldn't always get me to work. I didn't want a car. I liked keeping it simple. I enjoyed life, free and humble. Jersey knew something was going on. He didn't know exactly what, but he knew. Then, Jersey stepped up his mentoring from the physical to the spiritual plane."

"You almost done?" Liz asks, rubbing her hands together to fight the cold.

I stomp out my smoke and we return to the booth. Bill wants to hear more about the spiritual plane.

"He started out by taking me to magical places within the Pine Barrens. One was a deep, dark water hole. It was beautiful but eerie at the same time. We sat with our feet in the water, just taking in nature. An inner peace came, deep and pure like the water. Very quietly, Jersey started to hum a low drone or purr. It was contagious. I made the same sound without even realizing it. Other times, we went to a clearing at night. He would make me lay on my back and stare at the stars. Again, without realizing it, I was praying with my heart not my voice. So, the Jersey Devil is showing me inner peace. All of this brings me to a much higher plane spiritually and closer to God. A cursed devil teaches someone—me—who he thinks is an angel, but I am a cursed demon myself. The more I resolve who I really am, the more I learn to love nature and to have a closer relationship with God. I had to embrace terror to find peace, like so many paradoxes in life."

I shove cold fries in my mouth. Liz and Bill both look at me with question marks in their eyes. I know what they're thinking. They like my message, and they almost believe my story, but they can't buy it because of their understanding of the physical plane.

"Let me explain something. The physical plane of life is horizontal. Our knowledge and wisdom, you might say, the understanding of nature and the physical world, is flat. A horizontal plane. We learn this through science—knowledge, and our experience—wisdom. We have a preconceived understanding of things in our physical world. The spiritual plane is vertical, up and down. You hear things like, the spirit lifts you up and poorness of spirit brings you down. God is up, and the Devil is down. For me, the closer I become to nature, the more I'm in tune with the world around me. This includes people, birds, grass, trees, everything in our environment. The greater my spiritual understanding, the better I participate in life. A relationship, a friendship are spiritual things. Creativity is a spiritual thing. Helping someone is a spiritual thing. Being quiet can be a spiritual thing. And when the horizontal plane of nature and the vertical plane of spirituality meet, that's where you exist. That's where your little niche of life is. For that moment, life could be good or bad, up or down, full of love or full of fear...That's where you're at."

I have no way to know if they really understand what I was talking about but their attitude toward me remains the same—I think this guy is a bit crazy, but I like it.

"About two years ago, I feel this yearning to come home. I start following the Philadelphia news. I went to the library to look up obituaries to see who passed away in the old neighborhood. I would look up my old haunts like Walt's the King of Seafood at Second and Catharine, which is no more. I guess I started getting homesick. Jersey picked up on this, too. Did you ever hear the expression, 'dumb like a fox'? Well, the Jersey Devil is like that. In his shy and sly way, he pushed my attention to the North. Slowly, I started to realize that for some unknown reason, I needed to go to Philly and practice the skills I learned from Jersey. I wanted to return to my old neighborhood with the tools and understanding from the Pine Barrens."

Liz touches my hand. "You just left him? How sad."

"No, I didn't just leave him," I reply. "We made up our own symbols and sign language. For 'yes' and 'no' we use the same nodding and shaking your head. But for good, you rub your heart and nod. For bad, you would gesture like throwing something away and shake your head. The fact that he changed color to indicate his feelings was a great help, the same as my tone of voice. The word 'same' developed by placing two sticks that were the same side by side. It took a while for him to catch on but eventually he did. To ask a question, you put your arms out like a Y, making a face that expressed doubt."

"So, what do you mean?" Bill asks. "He doesn't sound 'dumb like a fox.'"

"He started to ask more questions about where I came from and how I came from out of the sky but couldn't go back. He could fly, and flying was natural to him. But for me to fly just one time and one time only is hard to understand. To him, I, too, was magical."

Bill puts his hand up.

"Flying in the sky from Philly to the Pine Barrens, how did that happen?" he asks.

"I don't know," I admit. "Sometimes I think it was a dream and other times I think it was a miracle but when it comes right down to it I just don't fuckin' know."

I finish the Coke. The ice long ago melted.

"I think Jersey knows," I say. "He knew it was time for me to leave. When I look back, I think Jersey planted the seeds for me to grow more homesick. He played dumb and let me think it was all my idea to return home. That's how he was dumb like a fox. When there are lots of questions and few answers, this jolts our soul and we realize that fact is not always truth. I felt at home in the Pine Barrens, but the truth is I needed to experience Philadelphia once more to see where I really belonged. It was just time for me to come back to Philly. I believe the Jersey Devil knew that much more than I did.

Again Liz folds her arms and leans on the table toward me.

"So, you just left."

"No. I didn't just leave," I repeat. "It took us a little while. I thought about it and decided I wanted to see the parade this year, I didn't think it was going to be so freaking cold. I went to the library and used the computer and found a hotel. The Philadelphia Hotel Bella Vista, it's over at Tenth and Catharine, pretty classy for me. I was lucky to get a room. I sold or got rid of all my stuff, didn't have much and I had some money saved. I packed a duffel bag, you know the kind with a long zipper on the side. Then on New Year's Eve, Jersey grew to the biggest I'd ever seen him. For the first time, I climbed on his back, sat just above the shoulders, threw the duffel bag across his neck right in front of me and grabbed on to his mane. He started to flap his wings. He leaped into the air and his huge wings started to push us upward into the night sky. Higher and higher we went until he put his wings out straight and we sailed across the sky like a huge Condor in flight. I thought we would fly north, directly to Philadelphia, but we didn't. Instead, we went southeast toward the shore. We must have come out somewhere between Sea Isle City and Avalon. Then Jersey dipped down low and flew just above the waves. You know the moon was almost full New Year's Eve and the night was clear, so you could see for miles. Dolphins jumped up out of the waves as if they were saying hello, it was incredible. I think Jersey did this just to show off and to give me this unbelievable memory. Jersey had turned a deep greenish blue to blend in with the night sky. The only thing that shined were his amber eyes. Even though it was 3°, I was warm, because right underneath me, he glowed a dull warm orange hue that warmed my whole body."

I stop and clear my throat. Liz and Bill are looking at me like two grade school kids listening to a story.

"Jersey sailed down along the coast past Stone Harbor, Wildwood, Cape May, and around Cape May Point. I'm thinking, 'I can't believe this. I'm sixty-four-years old flying on the back of the Jersey Devil, out over the ocean. The moon is full, the night is so clear I can see fireworks in the distance.' We went up the Delaware Bay past Wilmington and followed the river up to the city and landed in a vacant lot in South Philly. I climbed off his back and we stood there, looking at each other for a moment. I made the good sign. He did the same. A moment later, he was skyward. I watched him until he disappeared into the night."

"That's it?" Liz exclaims. "You're never going to see him again?"

"Of course, I'm going to see him again, Liz. When devils and angels become friends, they're friends forever."

Bill and Liz sit there with innocent smiles on their faces. There are no more questions just a peaceful silence. I get up and as I put on my coat, I thank them for listening, stick a folded twenty-dollar bill under my glass, and I walk out the door. As the cold hits me in the face, I wonder what Jersey is doing...

Lunch with Mom

I hold the door open and my Mom steps in, standing for a moment, as if she is surveying the seating arrangement. The familiar waitress waves us to a booth.

"Mom, do you want to sit in a booth?"

"Oh sure, a booth is fine."

We slide into our seats. The familiar waitress with kind, blue eyes sets down two glasses of water and two straws.

"I'll be back to take your order," she says as she hands us the menu.

Mom and I consider grilled cheese and tomato soup or crab patty and chicken soup. Mom picks crab patty and chicken soup. Returning, the waitress scoots into the booth and sits next to Mom. "It's good to be off my feet," she says.

With her kindness, she looks at Mom.

"So, how are you?"

Mom places her elderly hand upon the waitress's arm.

"Good," she answers, "and how are you?"

They chat for a minute as if they are old neighbors that met in a grocery store. I wait for the right moment and blow into the straw, launching the paper cover across the table and hitting my mother on the side of her face. Mom's eyes get big, and her mouth opens wide.

"Oh, you!" she exclaims.

The kind waitress laughs loudly and becomes embarrassed, putting her hands over her face. Mom turns, showing her stern, 'I mean business' face but can't keep up the charade and laughs. "He always does that," Mom says. "A grown man and still acts like a kid."

"I know but I'm still surprised every time he does it," the waitress adds.
Mom looks into her kind blue eyes.

"You know," my mom tells the waitress, "when you're my age you don't have to give a shit."

The kind waitress laughs and with gentleness pats the elderly hand, asking what she would like to eat. Mom looks at me and asks what it is I'm having. I order a crab patty sandwich, chicken soup, and applesauce. We will share fries.

"Oh, that sounds good," Mom says with a nod. "I'll have that, too."

As soon as the waitress leaves, Mom tells me that she is such a nice girl. Then, she asks if we ever ate at this diner before.

"Sure mom," I say. "That's Kristy, the waitress."

"Oh, that's right. I like her," Mom tells me with authority.

While having our soup, there's small talk of weather and chores that need to be done. She repeats at least three times that she needs to go to the bank.

"They do have good soup here," says Mom.

She arranges the cups on the edge of the table. Our meal arrives, Mom asks for 'some of that red stuff' for the crab cake.

"No problem, Hon," Kristy says. "I'll be right back with your cocktail sauce."

"Oh my God, look how big this is," Mom says.

"Just eat what you can, Mom."

"I can't eat all of this," she says. "You can finish what I can't eat."

"Okay," I assure her. "But eat as much as you can."

"This is enormous."

In between coaxing her to eat and the comments on the food, there is talk of family as Mom asks, several times, where my sister Peggy is. Kind Kristy the waitress congratulates my Mom on how much she ate.

"Well," Kristy adds. "You ready for dessert or coffee?"

"Coffee, no dessert," says Mom.

But Mom ends up with tapioca pudding, with whipped cream, and coffee. Taking the last two bites of her pudding, the look of being in the moment comes upon Mom's face.

"I've been thinking," she says. "What do you really think happens when you die? Do you really get to see people, like Dad and Nana and Pop-Pop or Jenny? I miss them. I really miss my parents."

"I think you'll get to see who you want to see," I tell her. "You could even see Abraham Lincoln."

"Oh, Abraham Lincoln, I don't even know him," she says. "But I really would like to see my family."

The spark leaves. She asks once more, "Where is Peggy?"

My mom returns to her confused adventure. Kristy, the truly kind waitress, bids us goodbye.

The Romance of Sneaker Sal and Freckled-Face Ray

When I was in junior high school, sometimes in the summer my friends and I would ride our bikes into town. We always ate lunch at Woolworth's, then played the pinball machines at Junior's Steak Shop. Sometimes, we fooled around at the junkyard underneath the bridge. We had to ride on Broad Street from Eighth Avenue to Second Avenue then over the bridge to get into town.

Returning home, we did the same but in reverse. Sometimes we would stop at the Yellow Lily Luncheonette at Sixth Avenue for a greasy hamburger and a Coke, and to buy cigarettes from the cigarette machine.

That's where I saw Freckled-Faced Ray for the first time. He was sitting at the counter sipping a Coke. He always sat at the very first seat of the counter near the cash register, so he could swing around on his stool and say hello to everyone that came in and goodbye to everyone that was leaving. You could tell that there was something different about Ray. We—my friends and I—referred to him as Freckled-Faced Ray, but everyone else just called him Ray.

The polite people would say things like "well he's a little, you know, different," or "he's a bit slow" or "peculiar."

And then others would say things like "he's a weirdo, but harmless" or "he's okay, strange but okay."

Then, there were the so-called straightforward and honest people that called him "a freaking retard."

They were just rude.

I guess at the time Ray was about twenty-five years old and lived with his mother on Sixth Avenue. He was always very neat and clean and it always looked like his mother dressed him. He stayed within the avenues. He never went beyond Eighth Avenue or below Fourth Avenue. But sometimes I would see him in the Rose Garden that was on the other side of Eighth Avenue.

All the neighbors knew him and looked out for him. The shop owners were kind and tolerant of Ray.

I once heard a man that was buying a lottery ticket say that Ray was good luck, and if Ray said "hi" to you, more than likely, you'd have a good day.

There was another neighborhood character that lived somewhere in the avenues, she was called Sneaker Sal.

Well, that's the only name I ever heard for her. She was thin, medium height and had straight black hair, shoulder length with bangs and a little greasy. She wore long full skirts with cardigan sweaters and of course, her trademark black high-top sneakers. Her sweaters were brightly colored, the colors reminded me of old-fashioned buttons my grandmother had in her button tin: yellow, red or a light green.

She was always walking at a quick pace like she was on a mission. In the summer, she had a big flat basket full of flowers: gladiolus, daisies, and hollyhocks. In the spring and fall, she carried a heavy-looking cloth bag with a flower print. In the winter, she wore a bright green or red full-length coat and held a brown paper shopping bag by the handles. She was a mystery.

There was a nervousness about her. If you got too close to her, her eyes seemed to shift back and forth, or she would give you a stink-eye look.

If a group of kids were walking toward her, she would cross the street. And the only time I heard her speak was when she told hecklers to "shut up" or to stay away from her.

It was only unavoidable that these two neighborhood characters would meet since their territories intertwined. They both had a strangeness and weirdness about them and people looked at them as an oddity. In this manner, they were very much the same.

But Sneaker Sal was fearful, standoffish, quiet and in constant movement. On the other hand, Ray was outgoing, loved to talk to people and could sit or stand in one place for hours.

At this time in my life, like most adolescents, I thought in black and white terms, right or wrong, same or different. I was pretty much the center of my universe.

So, when I thought of Sneaker Sal and Freckled-Face Ray, I put them into a category of weirdos as if they were missing emotions that included sentiments.

But there was one time— and only one time— that I witnessed Sneaker Sal and Freckled-Faced Ray sitting in the Rose Garden on the same park bench. I thought this to be strange but interesting. A paradox of weirdos. Could this be love?

I snuck up as close as I could get and spied from behind a tree. I couldn't really hear what was being said, but Ray was doing all the talking and I was sure that Sneaker Sal sat there with her eyes darting back and forth.

Then, Ray reached in his pocket and pulled out a pocket knife. Holding it flat in his hand, he showed it to Sneaker Sal. Very carefully, he took out each blade and held the knife in front of Sally. He pointed to each blade as if explaining the use of that particular blade. He then folded the blades back into the handle and handed the pocketknife to Sneaker Sal.

She held it in the palm of her hand and gazed upon it, a slight smile came upon her face. She then gave it back to Ray. He stood and put the knife back in his pocket. Sally stood and grabbed her bag.

Ray turned to the left and walked toward Eighth Avenue and Sally turned to the right and walked toward Ninth Avenue.

I leaned against a tree and watched the two of them walk away. I wondered if this was the beginning of a friendship or if this friendship had been going on for a while, or if it could be the end. They just walked away without looking back.

Now in my forties, I had the notion to stop at the Yellow Lily for breakfast. The layout was the same, but it was spruced up a bit. Nick wasn't behind the counter. Some young guy with a Mets baseball cap and a white apron was working the grill and the cash register, in the same way Nick did. I sat at the counter and a smiley-faced waitress with a Yellow Lily T-shirt and blue jeans poured me a cup of coffee and took my order.

The bell above the door jingled. The grill man and the waitress glanced over.

"Hi, Ray," they both said, almost simultaneously.

A gray-haired man hung his jacket on a hook and sat at the first stool at the counter. The smiley-faced waitress stood in front of him and very kindly asked how he was doing.

Ray nodded and said, "Okay."

I didn't have to study him or look very hard. I knew right off it was Freckled-Faced Ray. His sandy brown hair had turned to gray and his freckles had faded into faint wrinkles. But he still looked like his mother dressed him and his voice and mannerisms were the same as some thirty years ago.

"Are we having hot chocolate with cinnamon toast, Cheerios with bananas or English muffin with jelly and tea?" the waitress asked.

Ray thought for a minute. "Hot chocolate and toast."

"Sounds good to me, Ray."

And the waitress hustled to the hot chocolate machine. The bell above the door jingles and Ray turns around on his stool. He waves to the gentleman.

"Hi."

The man nods with a hello. Ray was still the official greeter at the Yellow Lily, saying hello and goodbye to all the patrons. If he knew someone's name, then they got the full treatment...asking about family, health, and their pets.

I ate my eggs slowly and sipped a cup of coffee. The whole-time I reminisced within my brain, catching glimpses of thirteen-year-old boys... being boys. I ordered a sticky bun and another cup of coffee just to linger longer. When Ray was finished with his hot chocolate and toast, he stood and fished a wallet from his back pocket.

Slowly, with great precision, he took out three dollars and laid them on the counter very neatly. He put on his jacket, stood by his stool, and said to the smiley-faced waitress, "Thank you, Maria."

She assured him that he was quite welcome. Then, he waved to the man at the grill.

"Thanks, Steve. See you later."

Steve wiped his hands on his apron. He came over and shook Ray's hand.

"Be careful out there, Ray."

Ray smiled his childlike smile and said okay.

I paid my bill and walked out onto the sidewalk, standing for a minute. I watched Ray walking toward Eighth Avenue. I don't know exactly why, but I put another quarter in the parking meter and followed a half block behind Ray. He led me to the Rose Garden and to the bench where he had sat with Sneaker Sal.

I gave him a couple of minutes to settle in and then I walked over.

"Hi, Ray," I said. "Is it okay if I sit down?"

He didn't say a word. He just nodded his head "yes."

I sat and there was complete silence for a minute or two. He turned to me and asked if I wanted to see his pocket knife. I said sure. From his pocket, he pulled out a shiny, worn pocket knife. He told me that his Uncle Bill had given it to him.

He pulled out all three blades and pointed to the big blade.

"This is for cutting."

He pointed to the littlest blade and told me it was for cleaning his fingernails. Then, he pointed to the broken blade and said that it used to be a screwdriver, but it broke. He folded the blades very carefully. Then he asked me if I wanted to hold it.

"Of course."

He handed it to me very gently. It laid flat in my open palm. I told him that it was a very fine pocket knife. With the knife still in the palm of my hand, I asked if he ever saw Sally, the girl that wore the sneakers. He took the knife from my hand.

"No," he said quietly. "She is gone."

We sat there in silence for a few minutes until Ray said he had to go. He got up and very slowly walked to Eighth Avenue. I stayed on the bench till my phone rang. It was one of my old friends from school. He wanted to know if we could get together for lunch some time. I suggested the Yellow Lily.

"I got out of my car and went into the diner. Making my way past the counter to the stool where I usually sit, brothers Danny and Donald conversed in deep discussion."
—TUESDAY AT THE DINER

Tuesday at the Diner

I pulled into the parking space and put my car in park. I stared out the windshield. Thoughts flood my brain and rapidly flow into one stream of thought.

I once heard or read that a famous writer, maybe Stephen King, would lay in bed at night telling himself a story until he fell asleep. The next morning, he would write what he liked or what he remembered from the story. I thought about this nighttime storytelling and realized that I had been doing it all my life. As a child, I would lay in my bed rehashing my day in story form. Many times, I would change the reality to where I was the hero of the story. The next morning, I would try to live my life like the story that I told myself the night before. Most times, I fell short of my expectations, not always, but most of the time.

I learned in philosophy class many years ago that Plato thought that man, as in "the human being," was made up of three things: reason, emotion, and appetite. Plato diagrammed this as a pyramid with the largest part, appetite, at the bottom. Emotion sat in the middle and the smallest portion reason at the top. Plato believed that we mostly lived for appetite: what we consume, what we like to do, and what gives us pleasure. Emotion comes next, the things that pushed our buttons: anger, compassion, sorrow, joy, fear, hope, gratitude, and jealousy. Emotions lead to action. The peak of the pyramid, and the smallest, was reason: the ability to think, understand and create a plan. Reason leads to knowledge.

In the early twentieth century, new-thought spiritual leader Emmet Fox spoke to thousands of listeners and wrote several books on the religious meaning of life. Doctor Fox suggests that there is more than one path to the great goal of our life. There is the pathway of knowledge, the pathway of action, and the shortest and easiest is the pathway of love.

I like the connection between Plato and Fox. It makes a lot of sense to me, but at the same time, I'm confused.

As much as I try, I cannot think my way through the journey of life. Knowledge can be a great gift, but it is motionless, not the driving force in my life. Action is movement charged by emotion; an exploit that can be swift or slow but needs knowledge or love to point the way. Our appetite tells us what we like by guiding our thoughts and emotional actions. But the true gift...the true path... the true creativeness behind knowledge and action is love.

If I'm guided by love, my journey will be joyful and my story will be true. Do I really believe this, or do I want to believe this? Or am I telling myself another bedtime story?

I got out of my car and went into the diner. Making my way past the counter to the stool where I usually sit, brothers Danny and Donald conversed in deep discussion. Danny and Donald were twins that look like brothers but not like twins. Danny was slender with thinning salt-and-pepper hair and Donald was a little hefty with thick gray hair. It is their eyes that are the same. They both have deep blue piercing eyes.

"A dog is funnier than a midget," Danny said.

"No way," replied Donald. "A midget is always funnier than a dog. Think about it. 'I look down and see a dog pissing on my knee' or 'I look down and see a midget pissing on my knee.' A midget is much funnier than a freakin' dog."

Danny shook his head 'no.'

"Two dogs," he said. "Let's make it two dogs. Two dogs are funnier than one midget."

"Then make it two midgets," Donald said. "Two midgets are funnier than two dogs."

"Two boxers are funnier than two midgets."

"No. Two poodles are funnier than two boxers."

"A boxer and a beagle. Think about it. 'A boxer is pissing on my knee and a beagle is pissing on my foot.' That's funny."

Donald looked at the ceiling and scratched his chin.

"A boxer and a beagle. Yeah, a boxer and a beagle may work if we have a midget, too."

He rapidly scribbled in his notebook. Ginny, the waitress, appeared with a cup of coffee and I ordered my lunch. I turned toward the brothers.

"A boxer, a beagle, and a midget are funny. But the two of you are funnier," I said.

Donald smiled.

"Thank you. It's good to know that comedy writers are appreciated," Danny said. "We do this out of love."

They really do love what they do, I thought.

To my right, Richard the hypochondriac sat two seats over and Ben, the quiet one, sat at his favorite perch. From this last stool at the corner, Ben can monitor the whole diner except the booth behind him, but he can usually hear the conversation.

Ben, a solitary man in his mid-fifties, always carried a book for his companion. A thick but neatly trimmed graying mustache accented his pale face. Hard to say what color his eyes were behind his dense, studious glasses. He always wore a tan baseball cap with Autobahn stitched across the front. Ben was a watcher and a studier. I would have said that he thinks his way along the path of life.

Now Richard, the hypochondriac, always told a story of disappointment and woe. Medical terminology and jargon rolled off his tongue as smooth as the lyrics of a song sung by Frank Sinatra. Violins played when he talked about his chronic sinus problem and his sciatic nerve discomfort. Richard wore a brown corduroy jacket that had shiny elbows and a light brown tweed cap that he got in Ireland. Sometimes he wore a tie, and on special feel-good days, he wore a bowtie. And today was a special day for Richard. He was seeing a new doctor, a new ear, nose, and throat doctor.

I heard a jolly "hello" and without turning around, I recognized the voice of Saint Teresa. She bustled down the aisle with her shopping bags and pockets bulging. The large red purse over her shoulder bounced off her hip and flapped in the breeze. She shuffled past and flopped her bags to the ground then scooched and wiggled onto the seat right next to Richard the hypochondriac.

A chuckle slipped out as I thought to myself, this ought to be good.

Teresa did not even pause and take a breath as she turned to Richard.

"How are you doing? You look terrible," she said. "Here, do you want one of these vitamins? They were givin' them away free at the clinic."

As she dipped her hand into the side pocket of her faded OD green field jacket, she continued. "How about some Aspergum? You know I think you need to do more exercise. You could lose a couple of pounds. Should you eat that pie on your plate? Get out in the weather."

Teresa's curly blondish-orange hair swayed as she looked over her purple framed glasses. She pointed her finger with a long, bright red fingernail that matched her lipstick.

"You," she said to Richard. "You of all people should know how to take care of yourself."

Richard's reddish complexion became a bit more rose-colored and he coughed. He reached for his glass of water. After a swallow, he recounted the tale of how and why he's going to a new doctor. Teresa and Richard become engaged in a conversation where they both voiced their own opinions and diagnosis of ailments. But neither one ever came close to the real disorder, a hearing disorder that they both have. They did not listen. Their actions pushed them through their lives.

And what was I doing here with this cast of characters?

It was Tuesday. And I ordered my lunch of tomato rice soup and a junior roast beef club sandwich. That's what I always ate on Tuesday. Or was it my path of love that brought me to this particular counter at this particular diner?

I know I think too much. But what really brought me there? Was it the conversation that stimulated my thoughts and the knowledge I received? Was this the action that I took to feel emotionally safe? I thought it was my appetite that brought me there, my appetite for life.

I loved going there and seeing my friends at the counter. I hope I was not the beagle or the boxer or the midget pissing on my own knee. Why did I doubt so much? Doubting the knowledge, the actions, the love, and that I am a part of this big universe that we live in? Why do I doubt the love I have for my fellow human beings? Why do I doubt the love I have for myself? Why do I doubt the love I have for God?

I know why I was there...I really loved the soup.

INSERT COIN OR
ParkCard TO DISPLAY
TIME PURCHASED
INSERT COINS
POM Inc. Russellville, AR USA
WWSH102

Twenty-Five Dollar Parking Ticket

William Sweetwater, better known as 'Billy Sweets,' looks at the meter and sees that there's only fifteen minutes left. He ups the time to an hour and fifteen and when he turns around, a street guy approaches him.

"Hey that's some tie you got on. Charlie Brown in a school bus. Yeah, the Peanuts kids riding in a school bus. That's a pretty cool tie," he says. "With a tie like that you got to have a sense of humor. I'll tell you what, for a dollar I'll tell you the two funniest jokes I know. Guaranteed to make you laugh and if you don't laugh, you don't got to give me a buck."

Billy looks at his tie and then at the street guy, who is probably in his 40s (but he looks like he is in his 50s). He's wearing an olive-green corduroy sport coat, which has a slightly ripped pocket and shiny elbows. He's disheveled and has a five-day growth of beard. The street guy sips his coffee from a styrofoam cup.

"What do you say? You want to hear two truly funny jokes for a buck?"

Billy shifts his weight into a more relaxed stance.

"What's your name?"

"Frankie," says the street guy.

"Well, Frankie, I'm about to go into the parking authority and pay a hundred and fifty-two dollars for a twenty-five-dollar ticket. Plus, you think my tie is funny. This tie was given to me by my students."

"Oh, no, man. I don't think your tie is funny. I think it's cool."

Billy smiles, and from out of his pocket he hands Frankie a dollar.

"I'll give you a buck, but you only have to tell me one joke."

Frankie squares off and his posture becomes more erect. He looks Billy in the eyes.

"What's the difference between a prostitute, a girlfriend and a wife?"

Billy smiles and offers a slight shake of his head.

"I don't know."

Frankie gives a little hand gesture and a smile.

"A prostitute says, 'Aren't you done yet?' The girlfriend says, 'Are you done already?' and the wife says, 'Beige, I'll think I'll paint the ceiling beige.'"

Billy laughs. He gives Frankie another two dollars.

"That was pretty good. You deserve a tip. I never met a panhandler with a routine like yours. Good hustle."

Frankie says thank you and then asks what Billy teaches.

Proudly, Billy says, "Music and Math."

Frankie draws his head back and peeks his eyebrows. "Music and math. Now that's funny."

"Why's that funny?"

"Music is fun and creative. Math is numbers and boring."

"No, no. They are both very mathematical, creative and fun. Did you ever hear a bandleader say, 'Here's a new number we would like to play,' or 'our next number is.' Why do you think he says that? Because music is by the numbers."

Frankie draws a puzzled look on his face.

"You're a jazzman. What's your name?" Frankie asks.

"Billy."

"You play cornet and fool around with the piano."

Billy nods. Frankie smiles and points his finger at him.

"I thought you looked familiar. You're Billy Sweets. The sweet sounds of Billy Sweets. Oh, man, Billy Sweets. What happened to you? You're a teacher? Man, I thought you'd be cutting records, playing in New York, Atlantic City, Las Vegas, L.A., Billy Sweets...Oh, man."

Billy laughs.

"During the day I am Mr. Sweetwater and at night I'm Billy Sweets. But who are you? Do I know you?"

"Yeah. You know me."

Then, with a big smile on his face Frankie puts his arms out palms up, as if to say ta-da.

"I'm Fearless Frankie."

"You mean that kid with the floppy hat that played tenor sax? Used to come to the jam sessions at Carter's Lounge and Fat Moe's?"

"That's me, Fearless Frankie."

With grins and laughter, they shake hands saying things like, 'holy shit, how long has it been,' 'it's good to see you,' and 'are you still hanging at Fat Moe's?'

"No..." then, Frankie says with concern in his voice, "but really...why are you a teacher?"

Billy hesitates, but then with a forcefulness in his voice he comes out with, "You know, life happens. No money, divorce, DUI, fear, anger and procrastination. I still struggle with procrastination. That's why my twenty-five-dollar ticket turned into a hundred and fifty-two-dollar ticket. I got backed into a corner. I had to find a real job and got this part-time teaching gig, which led into a full-time job. Turned out okay. I enjoy teaching. I still get to play some gigs and I do a little radio show on the PBS station. I'm okay, I'm having a good time. So, what about you? Are you still playing, Frankie?"

"No. Haven't played in years. Hocked my sax and tried to do some stand-up, but I kept falling down. Tell you the truth, Billy, I was never fearless, I was just high."

"I think the two-jokes-for-a-buck hustle is fearless. Still got some spark, Frankie."

"My spark is fading. But I make more money with two jokes for a buck than I ever did. Can you believe it?" he says. "And I don't have to pay any freaking income tax. The truth is, I got lost along the way and most of my money goes up my nose. I try to get my shit together, but I keep fucking up."

"Hey, let me go take care of this parking ticket. And when I come out, we'll go to lunch. I'm buying. But I want to hear the other joke first."

Frankie nods.

"A couple's been married for forty-five years. They're having some problems and they decide to go to a marriage counselor. The counselor asks what's the problem. The wife says, 'It's him. He's always picking his nose. I mean he picks his nose day and night and everywhere. Picks his nose at the dinner table, picks his nose when he drives a car, picks his nose in church and he picks his nose in bed. Always picking his nose.' The counselor then asks the husband if that is true and the husband nods and simply says, 'yes.' The counselor then asks the couple if there is anything else within the marriage that causes a problem. Once again, the wife pointed her finger at the husband and said, 'It's sex. We been married forty-five years and not once in the whole forty-five years did I get to be on the top.' The marriage counselor looks at the husband and asks if that was true. Once again, the husband nods and simply says, 'yes.' The counselor goes into a spiel about having a variety of sexual activity is healthy and asks the husband why he does not let his wife have the pleasure of being on top. The man leans forward and looks the counselor in the eye and says, 'When I was eighteen years old, my Uncle Theo gave me some good advice, and I adhere to it to this day...Keep your nose clean and don't fuck up!'"

When Billy comes out of the parking authority, Fearless Frankie is nowhere to be seen. Billy stands on the sidewalk disappointed and looks around.

He thinks to himself: I should have had lunch with him before I dealt with my ticket.

When Billy gets to his car, he sees a paper placed underneath his windshield wiper. He pulls it out and reads the handwritten note:

"Billy, it was really good to see you again. And I thank you for the offer of lunch. But it occurred to me it is time I take my own advice, 'Keep my nose clean and don't fuck up.'

Fearless Frankie

P.S. Hope to see you at Fat Moe's."

The Picnic

My grandparents always had a Memorial Day picnic for the official start of the summer. From what I remember, the typical Memorial Day picnic started with my Grandpa Fred squeezing the can of charcoal lighter fluid, making a constant stream of fluid while moving the can in a circular motion over the charcoal. He does this four or five times 'til there is a puddle of lighter fluid on the bottom of the grill. He then strikes a match and tosses it onto the charcoal. Poof! Flames shoot up and out and make a loud, whooshing sound. A cloud of black smoke rises and drifts past the open kitchen window.

My Grandmother Eleanor screams out the window.

"Fred, what the hell are you doing?"

Rubbing the singed hair on his knuckles, Grandpa looks up at the open window.

"I'm lighting the charcoal."

"With what, a flamethrower? It's only 11 o'clock."

"So?"

"People aren't coming until one o'clock."

"I want a nice bed of hot coals to cook on. Hey! Can you bring me a beer?"

"I just said it's 11 o'clock. No, I'm not going to bring you a beer."

"How do you want these chairs arranged?"

"Like we always do it, in a semi-circle."

That's the way it was when I was thirteen and it's pretty much the same way today, eleven years later.

Grandpa is a car salesman and co-owner of a used car lot, Uptown Auto, and Grandma worked at Binney and Smith in the crayon factory until she retired last year. They have been married forty-five years and for the past thirty, they've had a Memorial Day picnic. Always with the usual: hot dogs and hamburgers, potato salad, baked beans, beer and soda, watermelon, and Grandma's famous jellyroll lemon sponge cake with orange marmalade.

Eleven years ago, it was the usual gathering of friends and family. The first to arrive is always my family, Dad, their eldest son, Steve; my mom, Debbie; and daughter, Tiffany, that's me. Dad has always been some kind of computer guy. Mom is a travel agent. And, as Grandpa put it at that time, "Tiffany is a thirteen-year-old pain in the ass."

Next to arrive is Aunt Alice, who is called Muggsy, and her boyfriend Ramon. Aunt Muggsy is three years younger than my dad and a lot more free-spirited. At that time, she was waitressing at Mr. Bluster's Steakhouse and volunteered two days a week as a cook in a soup kitchen. Ramon is an artist who does abstract painting on old, recycled wood. He's all about color. At that time, Aunt Muggsy and Ramon had been dating for three years, but they had just moved in together a month before the picnic.

Next is usually Grandpa's brother, Uncle Billy, and Aunt Betty. Uncle Billy is older than Grandpa. He's red-faced with gray hair in a crew cut and loud. He loves to tease people and says funny sayings that I never understood, such as, "you talk like a man with a paper asshole" or "let's do it for shits and giggles," "that's better than a Snickers bar with marmalade," and "I got a case of the ass." Now, Aunt Betty is funny, too, but in a quiet way. She knew how to keep Uncle Billy in line.

Jack and Diane, who live next door to my grandparents, were always there. They were younger than Grandpa and Grandma, but they were real good neighbors and they all got along very well. Jack worked in the city planning office and also part-time at Granahan's Funeral Home. Diane is a special ed teacher.

This is the core of the picnic gatherers. My mom always makes her potato salad. Aunt Betty brings deviled eggs. Jack and Diane show up with a case of beer, a case of soda and a bag of ice. Aunt Muggsy provides the watermelon. Everyone helps out with the setup of the table and condiments and snack food.

Dad and Mom ask if there's anything they can do to help. Grandma directs Mom to put out the pickles, olives, and condiments.

Grandpa says, "Steve, why don't you go get us a beer?"

Dad returns with two beers.

"You know, Dad, I'm thinking it's time we get another car," he says to Grandpa. "The Ford Escort wagon is starting to get shabby. And I'm afraid of sinking money into it."

"We got a nice 2008 Dodge minivan and a two-year-old Subaru Outback."

My Dad rubs his short, well-cropped beard. "What color?"

Grandpa turns with a jerk. "What color? What the hell does color have to do with it?"

"You know, we want to look nice."

"Nice? For a computer geek, you really don't look at the practical side of things."

"I let you do that for me, Dad."

Grandpa sighs. "So, what do you think about your sister moving in with the artiste Ramon?"

"I guess it's okay. I hope they can make it financially. Oh look, here comes Uncle Billy."

Grandpa groans. "Already? Quick! Go get him a beer before he starts complaining about poor hospitality or some shit like that."

Dad goes to the ice chest to get Billy a beer and I come and stand next to Grandpa. He's looking at the charcoal and adjusting the air vent on the bottom of his grill. His prescription glasses turn dark from the sun, giving him a more authoritative look. He's wearing his official summer Hawaiian shirt with palm trees, pineapples and ukuleles. Grandpa's stomach is sticking out a bit and I poke his belly as I look up at him.

"Grandpa...Did Dad tell you I'm going to two overnight camps this summer? One for cheerleading and one for dance."

Grandpa looks at me with a scowl.

"Don't call me Grandpa."

"But you're my grandpa. What should I call you?"

"Call me Uncle Fred."

"That's silly. But I'm going away for two weeks, one camp for cheerleading and one for dance."

"What do you do in cheerleading camp?"

"We cheer."

"Is that all you do is cheer? You must walk around with a headache all the time."

"Grandpa, we go swimming, do crafts, sing songs and one night we have a talent show. I'm going to dance."

"Tiffany, do me a favor. Go in to Grandma. I mean Aunt Eleanor. Ask her for the hot dogs and hamburgers so I can put them on the grill."

I say okay and run into the kitchen. I remember telling my grandmother that Grandpa told me to call him Uncle Fred. She closes her eyes for a second and shakes her head.

"Your grandfather has a strange sense of humor, he thinks doing the contrary is funny."

"What do you mean 'contrary is funny'?"

"Contrary is like the opposite. For example, if I were to say, 'This pink blouse looks nice on me.' Grandpa would say, 'Purple will look better.' And if that got a rise out of me, he would think that was funny."

That's when I started to really understand my grandparents. They love to do battle, if they're not engaged in some kind of verbal combat they're not really happy. I used to think that they kept score of who won each battle. But it didn't matter who won, just so they were engaged in some bickering banter to prove that their thinking was better. They loved it and they didn't have to understand it.

I stare out the kitchen window. Grandpa looks to Uncle Billy and my dad who are talking. As I observe, I can tell Grandpa was in deep thought. I realize now that he was worried about Uncle Billy and his thoughts were probably something like, "Billy seems more wound up than usual. Maybe he was drinking before he came. Christ, I hope not."

There is a loud recognizable Harley-Davidson va-room in the driveway.

Grandpa says, "Eileen and Butch, the civilized bikers, are here."

Grandpa greets them in the usual way. "How's the bike running?"

Butch replies, "Good, good."

"We're fine too, Fred," Eileen says. "How's about you?"

Grandpa nods. "I'm fine. Things are good. Couldn't ask for a nicer day for a picnic."

Eileen is Grandma's sister, who is three years younger than Grandma. They look like sisters: same reddish-brown hair, same pretty brown eyes. Eileen is attractive but has a chiseled, tough look about her. Butch is five years younger than Eileen, he's forty-six with deep brown hair with a ponytail and a beard, a Harley tattoo with flames on his upper arm. Eileen and Butch met at work. Eileen is a secretary for a roofing company and Butch is a crew leader. They've been living together for ten years and they've been all over this country on Butch's motorcycle.

Grandpa has jealousy of Eileen and Butch. Deep inside he would love to travel out west on a motorcycle, but he's afraid to tell Grandma because she would think he's really crazy.

Jack and Diane walk in with a beanbag set. As they set it up by the side of the yard, Uncle Billy calls out a challenge.

"Beanbags. Steve and I will challenge anybody. Who's the first takers? Oh, Jack the undertaker and his lovely schoolteacher wife! Come on, Steve, grab two more beers and we'll take them on."

Jack and Diane look at each other with puzzlement. Jack shrugs his shoulders and without a word, they take on the challenge.

"Steve, I'll bring the beers over," my mom yells.

She grabs two beers from the cooler and walks to my dad and Uncle Billy. As Mom hands Uncle Billy a beer he smiles and says thank you. Uncle Billy has on red, white, and blue plaid madras shorts and a light blue T-shirt with a picture of a big bumble bee with a bib, holding a knife and fork. On the bib it says, "Bee Healthy, Eat Your Honey." His dark blue sneakers look brand-new.

My mom looks at Uncle Billy's T-shirt.

"Oh, you're eating healthy now?"

"Honey, I've been eatin' healthy for years," Uncle Billy responds.

"Oh, that's nice," my mom says in her naïve way.

Being thirteen, I had no idea what that innuendo was but I do recollect Uncle Billy teasing my dad and my dad being uncomfortable about it.

Grandpa goes into the kitchen.

"Where's the hot dogs and hamburgers?" he asks.

They don't realize that I'm sitting in the dining room around the corner out of sight, but I can hear their conversation. Grandma tells him it's too early to start cooking.

"Why?" Grandpa asks with frustration in his voice.

With a smart-alecky voice, Grandma replies, "Why? Because not everybody is here yet."

Grandpa mocks her. "Who's not here yet?"

Grandma lights one of her Virginia Slim cigarettes and blows the smoke with a sigh.

"Fred, you know who's not here yet."

"Who?"

"Dylan."

"Dylan. He could give a shit if we eat without him. He may not even come. I'm hungry. I'm starting the dogs and hamburgers."

Grandma hands over the plate of hamburgers and a pack of hot dogs.

"Oh, what's this crap about telling Tiffany to call you Uncle Fred?"

"I was just teasing her."

I can still imagine Grandma leaning toward Grandpa and pointing at him with two fingers that are holding her cigarette.

"You know she's too young to understand your weirdness," she says in a firm voice.

"I'm not weird. I just like to break balls."

"She's your granddaughter."

"No. I'm her Uncle Fred."

Grandpa walks out to the grill carrying the hot dogs and hamburgers.

When I return to the kitchen, I remember my grandmother asking me if I heard everything.

"Yes. I know Grandpa's a big tease," I answer. "I think some of the things he says are funny and some of the things I don't understand. But I like being around him. He doesn't talk to me like a kid. I know Uncle Dylan's always late and that people worry about him. I guess everybody wants him to do better. I like him the same way I like Grandpa."

At the time, I was just as surprised about what I said as my grandmother was. She comes over to me and kisses me on the cheek.

"Tiffany, you are growing up. Keep growing in that direction."

She hands me a plate of cold shrimp with cocktail sauce and whispers that it was a surprise. I got the honor to put it on the table. When I present it to the table, everybody flocks around like seagulls after spilled french fries on the boardwalk.

"Oh, Tiffany, this is great!" they say.

When everybody gathers their food and claims a place to sit, Grandma quietly tells Grandpa to save a hot dog and hamburger for Dylan.

Grandpa smiles.

"Okay, Aunt Eleanor."

Grandma gives Grandpa the look of 'I mean business.'

"Stop that shit," she says.

Grandpa sits in a chair adjacent to the picnic table so he can see and converse with everyone. He has a TV tray in front of him to set his food and drink upon, which gives him a child-like look. At the picnic table are Tom and Joanne, old friends of Grandpa. They all went to high school together. Tom and Joanne have an insurance business. Over the years, Grandpa and Tom gave a lot of work to each other by recommending each other to their customers. Tom has a nickname of Bumps because when he started out in the insurance business, he sold a lot of car insurance. His clients would say, "It was just a bump, it shouldn't be too expensive." And somehow the nickname stuck. The only one who really calls him that is Uncle Billy.

Mary and Mary Lou are also sitting at the table. Mary was a coworker of Grandma's at Binney and Smith and Mary Lou did Grandma's and Aunt Eileen's hair. Mary and Mary Lou have been friends for a long time.

They both are dog people. Mary has two Yorkshire Terriers, Oscar and Wilma. Mary Lou has a chocolate lab, Bosco. If they're not talking or showing pictures of their dogs, then they're telling of their latest cruise. This is right up my Mom-the-travel-agent's alley. She asks how their Caribbean cruise was. In less than a minute, Mary brings out her phone and they are engrossed with laughter and conversation.

Mary and Mary Lou don't live together, but it is often wondered if they are more than friends. It's an unsaid don't-ask don't-tell policy. Everyone accepts and respects them...That is, except Uncle Billy.

Sometimes Uncle Billy nudges the conversation into the direction of "are they or are they not lesbians?"

Then Grandma pulls him aside. "What? Do you think your shit is ice cream? Stop antagonizing, Billy. Leave them alone. They're nice women."

Uncle Billy nods and simply says, "I'm sorry."

But that doesn't stop him from busting somebody else's chops. He sees Diane biting into a hot dog and immediately Billy sings out the line from John Cougar Mellencamp's Jack and Diane song, "Suckin' on a chili dog outside the Tasty Freeze." He continues on singing the song but he ends with "a little ditty 'bout Jack and Diane, the want-to-be undertaker and the special ed teacher!"

Grandpa waves his hand.

"Bill, nobody wants to hear you sing," he calls out, "and I know the money Mom gave you for singing lessons, you spent on cigarettes."

Billy laughs and Betty, Billy's wife, motions to him to come sit next to her. Bill and Betty have been married a long time, and they're both 62 years old. Bill is five years older than Grandpa and his hair is much whiter. He's the same height as Grandpa, 6 foot, but a little heftier, more on the pudgy side. He's a union electrician soon to retire, and Betty thinks that he is fearful to retire.

Betty is quiet but very much aware. She had a heart attack two years ago. Quit smoking, drinking and keeps herself in shape by going to the gym. She's very worried about Bill when he retires. With his personality, she can see him in the local clubs, getting drunk, spouting off and getting himself in trouble. At least, that's what I overhear her telling Grandma.

Uncle Billy walks over to Betty.

"Listen, honey, I got to see a man about a horse and some manure. I'll be right back."

Billy goes into the house, headed for the bathroom.

Dylan suddenly appears next to Grandpa.

"Any more hamburgers left?" he says. "I'm starving."

Grandpa gets up from his chair.

"I'll put one on, it'll only take a minute or two."

They walk over to the grill.

"I'm glad you came," Grandpa says. "Your mom is worried about you."

Dylan smiles and pushes his long brown hair to the side.

"I know she worries. But I'm okay."

"You working?"

"Yeah. Still landscaping, cutting grass and shit for Ben."

"Ben?"

"Yeah, he's the guy that owns Perpetual Care Landscaping."

Grandma sees Dylan. She quickly comes over with her arms open. She hugs him and kisses him on the cheek.

"Oh, Dylan, I'm so glad you came. I see your dad is making you a hamburger. Should I fix you a plate?"

"No, Mom, I can do it."

"Oh, it's so good to see you.'"

She kisses him on the cheek again.

A cry of "Dylan" rings out. Dylan turns to look and sees Muggsy waving him over.

Grandma gently puts her hand on his back. "Go ahead over and see your sister. I'll bring your plate."

Dylan nods and hurries across the patio. Grandma looks at Grandpa and in a soft voice she asks, "Do you think he's okay?"

"Yeah I do. He said he's still working, doing landscaping. Eleanor, you got to remember you have two other kids."

"Of course, I know that. Why would you say that?"

"I'm just saying. Go ahead, fix his plate. This hamburger is about done."

Aunt Muggsy, Ramon and Uncle Dylan are gathered in a cluster of chairs alongside the patio. Now that I'm older, I can imagine what was said in their conversation.

"Dylan, I'm really happy you came," Muggsy says, "I haven't seen you since Easter."

Then, she giggles.

"Are you still cutting grass or selling grass?"

Dylan smiles. "Both, but mostly cutting grass. And I've been playing with the Rocket Rangers."

"I saw them at the Fun House once," Ramon says. "They were a pretty good band."

Dylan nods. "Yeah, Jimmy Sykes, the leader, kind of regrouped and asked me to play rhythm guitar and sing backup."

"Cool," says Muggsy.

"I played with them at two gigs now. It seemed to go pretty well. We're going to be playing First Friday somewhere. And there's talk about opening up for some hot shit band at the Roxy."

Ramon looks surprised.

"Way cool," Muggsy says.

Grandma arrives with Dylan's plate.

"Here you go, honey. I put a couple of Aunt Betty's deviled eggs on. I know how much you like them. Beans, some sweet gherkins, and chips."

"I can see, Mom. You don't have to give me a commentary."

Muggsy laughs. With disapproval, Grandma looks at Muggsy and then at Dylan.

"You don't have to be such a smart ass," she scolds him.

Dylan closes his eyes for a second.

"I'm sorry, Mom. I do appreciate you making me this plate."

"Well, you should," she replies. "I think your dad is worried about Uncle Billy. Maybe you guys should keep an eye on him."

Muggsy shrugs her shoulders.

"Uncle Billy is Uncle Billy," she says. "He's always been a lovable pain in the ass."

"Oh honey, you're right," Grandma says, "but your dad senses there is more to it. You know how siblings can be. You guys know shit about each other before I do."

Ramon laughs. Then, to cover up his laughter, he says, "You got a point there."

Grandma gives Ramon the "maybe it's time for you to shut up" look.

"We'll just keep an eye out for Uncle Billy," she says. "Oh, I got to give this recipe to Joanne. It's my lemon sponge jellyroll. Don't forget to talk to your brother."

Grandma hustles off to the picnic table.

"Mom is still a trip," Muggsy says. "Don't you think it's a little weird? Her saying that about Uncle Billy?"

Steve steps into the group. "What's a little weird?"

Muggsy looks up. "Mom asking us to keep an eye on Uncle Billy, that Dad's worried about him."

"I was playing bean bags with him before. He seemed like Uncle Billy. He might be getting a cold. He was sniffing and wiping his nose."

"Now you're Doctor Steve," Dylan says.

"Hi, Dylan."

Dylan smiles. "Yes."

Steve nods his head. "Figures you would come to Mom and Dad's high.

"Stop," Muggsy says. "Steve, pull up a chair and join us."

"No. Tiffany and I are going to play bean bags against Jack and Diane. Talk with you later." Steve walks over to the beanbags.

Muggsy looks at Dylan. "Why do you always have to start shit? Steve's okay."

"Oh, he's like fucking Fred Junior."

In a calm voice, Ramon says, "Sometimes older brothers are like that. I know I can get that way."

"You're not as big a prick as he is."

"Ramon is showing at the Talbert gallery for the month of June," Muggsy says, maybe not so randomly. "Then in July, we'll be doing a show in York and one in Baltimore."

Dylan smiles. "Hey, that's really good."

The family dynamics between siblings is strange and exclusive. The differences make the unity. As an only child, I could never understand the jealousy and resentments between my father and his brother and sister. It was easy to see that Aunt Muggsy, the female middle child, was the peacekeeper; my dad was the oldest son, the achiever; and Uncle Dylan, the youngest, was the mascot and wanderer. Today, even though they are older and more mature, they still have hurting wounds from family battles.

Aunt Betty comes running out of the back door screaming.

"Something's wrong with Bill! Something's wrong! Bill's not moving!"

Grandpa gets up. "Where is he?"

"The bathroom," yells Betty.

Grandpa runs in the back door with her, my dad follows right behind them. Grandpa reaches the bathroom and stares at his brother sitting on the toilet, pants down to his knees, slumped over and motionless.

"For Christ's sake, Bill," Grandpa calls out. "You fucking passed out on the toilet."

Grandpa shakes him, but Uncle Billy just falls to the side.

"I think it's more than Uncle Billy being passed out," my dad says. "We better call an ambulance."

My dad steps into the hallway and brings out his cell phone. With a shaky hand he pushes 9-1-1.

"I want to report an emergency."

Grandma approaches the bathroom door and sees Grandpa slapping Billy's face.

"Just what in the hell is going on here?" she hollers.

Dad motions for her to be quiet. Grandpa turns around.

"He might be dead."

Grandma lets out a loud and long, "ooooh, my God."

"Go get Jack," Grandpa says.

Grandma turns and runs to the back door. Calling for Jack, she motions for him to come.

"Check Bill out," Grandpa says. "I think he's dead."

"Me?" Jack replies.

Grandpa nods.

"Yeah, you're like a half-assed undertaker. Come on see what you think."

Grandpa steps aside so Jack can get to Billy.

"I'm an apprentice, that's a helper to the undertaker."

Jack tries to feel his pulse and asks for a small mirror to stick under his nose. Grandma motions and tells him to look on the shelf. Jack finds a hand mirror and puts it under Billy's nose.

"I don't see anything."

Grandpa sighs.

"Well?" Grandpa asks impatiently. "What do you think? Is he dead?"

Jack turns and nods to Grandpa and Grandma.

"It appears that way."

Grandpa shakes his head.

"Pull his pants up," Grandpa tells Jack.

"Me?"

"Yeah. You're the undertaker guy here. You're used to working with dead people. Pull his pants up."

"I'm going to need some help."

The doorbell rings and my dad answers the door. Two police officers ask if there is an emergency here? Dad tells them yes and that they should follow him. When they get to the bathroom, Grandpa and Jack are trying to pull up Uncle Billy's pants.

"What are you doing?" one of the police officers asks.

"What does it look like?" Grandpa says. "We're trying to pull up his pants. My brother is dead."

"We'll take care of it," the other police officer says. "Just leave everything the way it is."

Grandpa looks at the police officer.

"He's my brother. I don't want him sitting here with his Willie Johnson hanging out."

"Sir. It will be fine; the paramedics will be here any moment. Would you please step out of the bathroom, sir?"

"Why don't you give us a hand?" Grandpa asks.

Now it's back to the original police officer.

"Sir, would you please step out of the bathroom? We would like to have everything just the way it is."

There is a pause. Grandpa and the police officer stare at each other.

Once again, the officer says, "Sir, would you please step out of the bathroom."

Grandpa puts his hands up, motions with his head for Jack to leave, and Grandpa walks out of the bathroom. One of the officers gathers Dad, Jack, Grandma, and Grandpa and puts them in the living room. Then, he goes outside to the picnic and asks that no one leave. Betty is sitting with Tom and Joanne, sobbing. She asks the police officer if her husband is all right.

"The paramedics will be here any moment and then we'll know more," the police officer says. "I think it's best if you just stay out here with your friends."

Tom and Joanne agree with the officer and they get Betty to sit. The other officer secures the body and calls for the coroner. Grandpa stands by the doorway of the bathroom. The police officer looks at Grandpa.

"Sir, would you please go into the living room and have a seat."

"Did you call the coroner?" Grandpa asks.

"Yes."

"How long will it take for him to get here?"

"About a half hour to forty-five minutes," the officer says. "Would you please go in the living room and have a seat?"

The other officer enters the hallway.

"I'm Sergeant Briggs and this is Officer Sotack," he says to Grandpa. "I'm sorry. It seems confusing, but we had to secure the area."

The sergeant glances at the officer as if he has a question and the officer nods.

"Officer Sotack called the coroner."

"I know that and it's going to take at least a half an hour for him to get here," says Grandpa. "My sister-in-law is sitting out there, more than likely praying hope-filled prayers, while her dead husband is sitting on the commode."

The sergeant nods.

"Yes, sir, that's our next step," the sergeant says. "Would you like to tell your sister-in-law that her husband has passed or would you prefer that we do it?"

"I guess it would be best if my wife and I tell her," Grandpa says in an apologetic tone, "but maybe it would be good if you are present, too."

"Okay, we'll bring her into the living room," the sergeant says, "but I don't think it's a good idea for her to see the body."

Betty comes into the living room.

"I know he's dead. I know Bill is dead," she says. "I just need someone to tell me it's so."

Taking her hand, Grandpa nods.

"Yes, Betty, Bill has passed."

Betty sits down, tears flow.

"I knew it. I knew he was worried about retirement. It was just too much for him."

She puts her face into her hands and allows the shock and sorrow to pour out of her. The coroner arrives and things become very professional and serious.

"It seems like we're in a movie," Grandpa tells Grandma. "I can't believe this is happening."

After a while, the coroner and Sergeant Briggs walk into the living room. The sergeant holds up a plastic bag with a little vile of cocaine inside. He looks at Grandpa.

"What do you know about this?"

"About what?" Grandpa answers.

The sergeant slightly shakes the bag.

"About this vial of cocaine. We found it in his pants pocket."

Then, he looks directly at Aunt Betty.

"Mrs. Stevens, do you know anything about this?"

"Cocaine," Grandpa repeats. "You gotta be shittin' me."

Betty shakes her head. "No. Bill never did cocaine."

The coroner takes a half step forward. "Since we found the cocaine, the death will be considered suspicious and an autopsy will be done. The officers will be questioning you and the guests. We will remove the body shortly."

Sergeant Briggs and Officer Sotack, as quickly as they could, ask everyone a few questions. Within a half an hour the police, the coroner, and Uncle Billy are gone.

My dad and mom take Aunt Betty home. She tells them she just wants to be at home and sit in her chair with her cat, Priscilla, on her lap. I stay at the picnic because I want to know more about Uncle Billy's death.

"I can't believe this shit is happening," Grandpa says, growing angry. "Where the hell did Billy get cocaine?"

Everyone is seated on chairs or at the picnic table. I'm tossing bean bags by myself, so I'm not in the way, but I can still hear and see what's going on. Sitting at the edge of the patio, Grandpa scratches the back of his head and slowly looks at each individual. You could see the wheels turning in Grandpa's mind. I believe he was strategically trying to eliminate who might have something to do with Billy's cocaine use.

It looks as though he is thinking to himself, "Jack and Diane...no. Tom and Joanne...naw. Eileen and Butch...maybe Butch. Mary and Mary Lou...I doubt it. Muggsy and the artiste, Ramon...Yes and no, it could be Ramon...Dylan...I hate to say it, but he is the most likely."

Grandpa approaches Dylan.

"What do you know about Uncle Billy having cocaine?"

Dylan raises his eyebrows.

"Cocaine? What the hell do you mean cocaine?"

"Uncle Billy had a vial of cocaine in his pocket. I want to know where he got it."

"Sure. Right away you come to me."

"Dylan, I'm not stupid. I know when you cut Uncle Billy's grass, you smoke a little pot with him."

"So, what does that have to do with cocaine?"

"They're both drugs. They are both illegal."

"Anything that has to do with drugs or being illegal, I'm the go-to guy, right?"

Tom interrupts. "Fred, come over here a minute. I want to talk to you."

Grandpa jerks his head and looks at Tom. "What the hell?"

Tom takes Grandpa by the arm.

"Listen, Fred, Dylan had nothing to do with this," Tom says. "Come on, step over here, I want to talk to you."

"You want to talk to me?"

This is what I think happened after hearing, over the past eleven years, what my family says about the conversation Tom and my grandfather had. I got one story from Aunt Muggsy, a story from my mom and dad, and grandma never said much about it. What I think is the truth mostly came from Grandpa himself, although I never heard Tom's version of the story.

They walk over to the side of the house. Tom takes a deep breath.

"Just hear me out, Fred, and try not to interrupt."

"What the fuck are you talking about? Get to the point."

"About six months ago, I took Billy to a poker game at Spuds Zabriskie's house."

"Spuds Zabriskie. What the hell are you doing at a poker game at that scumbag Zabriskie's house?"

"Just hear me out. Billy wanted to get into a game that had a little higher stakes. And you know not everybody can take Billy, but Zabriskie's crowd could, from knowing Billy from the old days. About once a month, I would go over to Spud's to play seven card draw. So, one night I took Billy. He did good, he won about four hands. But some of the guys were doing cocaine and they gave Billy a taste."

"Oh, Jesus Christ, Tom."

"Yeah, I know, I know. Anyway, Billy was doing good with the cards. Sometimes he would lose, but most of the time he won."

Grandpa put his head down and brought it up quick, looking Tom in the eye. "And he spent all his winnings on cocaine."

"I don't know why, but Billy was all screwed up over this retirement shit."

"That's right, Tom. This is shit. I think it's time you leave."

"Come on, Fred. You know how Billy is."

"No, I know how Billy was. Now just get the fuck outta here."

Tom walks away looking at the ground, shaking his head, gathers up his wife, Joanne, and without saying goodbye they walk out the gate. Grandpa goes over to Dylan and tries to apologize, but Dylan won't have any of it. Muggsy takes Grandpa by the arm and tells him to go inside with Mom. She and Ramon, Eileen and Butch would clean up. And that's how the picnic ended.

Three months later at the Labor Day picnic, Grandpa and I are sitting at the picnic table playing the board game Parcheesi. As I move my red man four spaces, without looking up, I say, "I'm in high school now."

Grandpa scratches the back of his head. "I thought you were in middle school."

"I was in middle school. In two weeks, I'll be fourteen and I'm in ninth grade."

"Ninth grade is in high school?"

"Yes."

"It wasn't that way when I was a kid. Ninth grade, you were still in junior high school."

"Now in ninth grade you are a freshman starting high school."

"Fourteen, I thought you're twelve."

"No, Grandpa. I'll be fourteen."

"Fourteen. Where have I been for the past two years?"

"Right here, like always. Oh, where's Aunt Betty? I thought she would be here."

"She's working at the country club, tending bar and flirting with old duffers."

"Old duffers? What the heck is a duffer?"

"A duffer is an old guy that likes to play golf and then sit at the bar and tell stories about it."

"Do you think Aunt Betty really flirts with duffers?"

"Yeah, why not? She's not married now."

"Sorry, Grandpa, I just landed on your man. You go back home."

"Every time that happens it feels like my man's been put in jail."

"I feel sorry for Uncle Billy."

"Do you feel sorry or do you feel sad?"

"I guess both. I feel sorry that he didn't live longer and I feel sad that he's not here."

"He sure went out in a true Billy way. I think he's still laughing about it."

"You really think that he thought it was funny that he died on the toilet?"

"Of course, he did. Uncle Billy lived by his feelings. That's why he had so many bad habits, he did things because they felt good. His autopsy showed that he died from a heart attack, maybe it was brought on by the cocaine and maybe it wasn't. But his search for feeling good didn't do him any good. You know, Tiffany, sometimes life is like being lost in the forest. You know, you come to a point where you must pick a direction to go in. Most people think about their choices and put things in some kind of order and find a clear and safe direction out of the forest. But Uncle Billy would come to that point where he had to pick a direction and say, 'Oh, this feels good!' And that's the direction he would go in."

"But why is he laughing?"

"His feelings and his bad habits kept him going in circles. And when he thought he was on the right path, it led him to a bathroom, where he had to sit on the toilet to relieve his excess waste. But instead of going he went and ended up leaving the forest forever. I know he would think that to be quite humorous."

It's been eleven years since the passing of Uncle Billy. The Memorial Day picnics are pretty much the same. My Mom and Dad are the first to arrive with mom's potato salad. Jack and Diane still live next door and bring beer, soda, and ice. Aunt Muggsy brings her traditional watermelon, but now she's married to David, a psychologist, but Grandpa doesn't know if he likes him because he wears socks with sandals. Eileen and Butch are always there, but their motorcycle road trips had to end since Butch had back surgery. Mary and Mary Lou live together and run an animal shelter for unwanted dogs called The Stray Dog Lodge. Uncle Dylan still comes late and he went to college and became a biology teacher.

For the past five years, Aunt Betty has been engaged to Walter, a retired Jack Daniels salesman and ex-golf pro. She still brings her deviled eggs. Grandma and Grandpa are still doing verbal combat but age has mellowed them out a bit.

Grandpa keeps a photo of Uncle Billy on the shelf above the toilet with a little plaque that says, "In honor of Bill, instead of going, he went." Grandpa also likes to tell people that the bathroom is haunted. Tom and Joanne don't come anymore. Grandpa never talked to Tom since Uncle Billy died. And me, I went to school for journalism and work for a struggling newspaper. I still love to have my little talks with Grandpa.

Magic Pies

I knew an old Pennsylvania Dutch woman, Grammy Boyer, who could make the absolute best pies. She could roll out a pie crust at sonic speed, the whole time telling you a story about her little dog that got in trouble in an outhouse, by relieving himself on the toilet seat.

She then laid that pie crust in the pie plate, trimmed the edge with a knife, and crimped the dough in a flawless design only stopping a moment to sip some coffee. Then, she went into another story about her and her husband, Walter, vacationing in Florida.

"Ock," she said, "It was so darn hot down there. I couldn't wear my girdle. Oh, it made me feel so loose. Why that Florida is not for me."

Every time her crust was flaky and light, nothing but perfection. Her fruit pies had the flawless balance of sweetness and a touch of tart. Cream pies were heavenly. The meringue peaked like sugary mountains. When she made shoofly pies and funny cakes, the gooey bottoms stuck to your tongue while the cake melted in your mouth. A culinary marvel of magical baking.

The magic didn't stop with the taste of her pies. It was the way you felt when you were in Grammy Boyer's presence, as if you had known her for years. She would tell stories about milking a cow for the first time and getting milk all over her stockings and shoes and not much in the bucket.

When she told about her brother Willie passing gas in church, you laughed 'til the tears of humor came flowing from your eyes.

There were tears of sorrow that rolled down your cheeks when she spoke about losing her second child to what she called 'crib disease.' It seemed that she baked in a secret charm that pleased the soul as well as the tongue.

Yes, I would say that the pies were pleasing to your very soul. For when one ate a piece of Grammy Boyer's pie, the enjoyment went beyond the taste buds—a feeling of deeper fulfillment, as if your tongue could taste Grammy's stories.

Oh, Grammy Boyer was clever. I remember a time when two of her neighbors were feuding. Mrs. Schneck and Mrs. Greenawalt had a dispute over a fence and a wash line. It seemed that Mrs. Schneck's fence would catch the sheets and dresses of Mrs. Greenawalt when a breeze blew, soiling them and in one case, tearing the hem of her dress. Well, Grammy Boyer invited them both over for pie and coffee. She made a special pie, a strawberry-rhubarb tart. She told me that she chose the strawberry-rhubarb tart because it takes a lot of sugar to balance out the tartness of the fruit. But when the proper amount of all the ingredients is blended together and baked at the right temperature for the right amount of time you get a pie that is perfect for two feuding friends. The bitterness is combined with the sweetness and the harshness fades.

So, the sweetness of their longtime friendship overcame the bitter harshness of their disagreement. Mrs. Schneck lowered her fence a bit and Mrs. Greenawalt moved her wash line to the other side of the walkway.

And every spring they visit Grammy Boyer for strawberry-rhubarb tart, and a story that tickles their funny bones and tugs at their hearts.

Yes, I would say that there is magic in Grammy Boyer's pies.

The only person I knew to say an unkind word about Grammy Boyer was the Reverend John J. Ziegenfuse. It must've been about ten or twelve years ago, in a conversation with Irene Schmidt, when the good reverend referred to Grammy Boyer as an old Powwow Witch, and that her do-gooding was just a façade.

Why he would say something like that, heaven only knows.

This offense got back to Grammy Boyer by way of Mrs. Schneck, and Grammy just shrugged her shoulders.

"Everybody has their opinion," she said.

A year later the Reverend's wife ran off. You need to know that the Reverend's wife was Marianne Bowser, she was the head cheerleader, Prom Queen, and voted the most likely to succeed. Marianne went to college, made the Dean's list, and got a degree in social work. She was very pretty, outgoing, and did a lot of charity work for the community. Everybody liked Marianne.

A lot of people would say, "I just don't understand why Marianne would marry a stuffed shirt like Reverend Ziegenfuse" or, "What she sees in him is beyond me" or "He is a handsome man and he can be personable, but he's as rigid as a wsshboard."

It was a year after the Reverend badmouthed Grammy Boyer, at the church's spring social, that Grammy made sure that Marianne ate a piece of her coconut cream pie.

Now, some say soon after Marianne ate that coconut cream pie, she started to change. It wasn't a drastic change. It was subtle. She started to poke fun at the Reverend, smiled a lot more at the men in the congregation. She had a much more carefree attitude.

Then, one day, she was gone. Nobody saw her leave and nobody ever heard from her either. The Reverend was distraught, only preached on Sundays and the rest of the time he was scarcely seen.

Slowly he came out of his shell. As Budd Johnson says it, "He became more tight ass than ever."

There were rumors about Marianne. Sally Wagner's nephew, George, insisted he saw her when he went to see a Broadway show in New York. She was one of the dancers in the show, and that she even winked at him. Others say she ran off with Buck Taylor, a local musician, and went to Nashville. Sadie and Charles Ostroff swear they saw her at a diner in New Jersey, eating coconut cream pie with two sailors.

Now a year ago, the local fire hall was putting on Drag Queen Bingo for a fundraiser. This ruffled Reverend Ziegenfuse's feathers. He was quoted in the local Community Times, "This is an abomination. One would think that the officers of the volunteer fire company would have better moral standards and could come up with a much more wholesome way to raise money for the fire department."

Privately, amongst the members of the congregation, he said, "Bingo is gambling and that's something that the Catholics do, a UCC church community would never do that. As far as the drag queen business, that's promoting homosexual behavior and that is just wrong."

Pete Peterson, the fire chief, was quoted saying, "We make more money with drag queen bingo, than twenty bake sales and any amount of cars passing by putting money in a boot."

On the night of the bingo fundraiser, the fire hall was packed and things were moving along smoothly. Two games of bingo were played and then a break with one of the Queens doing a song. There was Marilyn Monroe singing "Diamonds are a Girl's Best Friend," Dolly Parton singing "9 to 5," and Barbra Streisand singing "People."

Of course, there were refreshments: pork barbecue, hot dogs, French fries, coffee and soda, as well as baked goods. Grammy Boyer supplied apple pie, shoofly pie, and funny cake.

At the start of the evening, Grammy Boyer told Mrs. Greenawalt's nephew, Tom: "Now, if Reverend Ziegenfuse would happen to come in, you make sure that he gets a piece of this funny cake. Now, mind you, you have to give him a piece of this funny cake and make sure he takes a bite."

Tom gave Grammy a puzzled look.

"He'll never come to Drag Queens Bingo," he said.

She smiled.

"You never know what a man like him will do," she replied.

It happened right when Barbra Streisand started to sing "People." The good Reverend walked in and stood by the refreshment counter. People slowly moved away, giving him a wide berth. Just as Grammy Boyer requested, Tom went over with a piece of funny cake.

"Hi, Reverend, I'm a little surprised to see you here."

The Reverend smirked. " So am I."

He held the funny cake just below the Reverend's chin.

"Would you like some funny cake?" Tom asked in a welcoming voice.

"No."

Tom was not coached to say this, but it was genius what came out of his mouth.

"Oh, my Mom made this," he said. "If you don't have some, I'm sure you would hurt her feelings."

The Reverend smiled. He took a big bite of the funny cake. Instantly, Reverend Ziegenfuse's expression changed. He stared at Barbra Streisand. He took another bite of the funny cake and smiled, not his usual polite smile but a genuine smile.

He walked to the edge of the tables, staring at Barbra Streisand still singing "People." And when the song was over, nobody clapped harder or gave a louder "woo, woo" yell than the good Reverend Ziegenfuse.

A week later, the reverend was seen with Barbra Streisand having coffee at the Dunkin' Donuts. It was less than six months after that, that St. John's Church opened its doors to the LBGTQ community. Whenever the church had a bake sale, the reverend personally asked Grammy Boyer if she would bake some pies.

Would you say there is magic in Grammy Boyer's pies?

TELEPHONE
TELEPHONE

Phone Call in the Rain

He stood outside the apartment building in the rain, looking up at the light in the second-floor window. He darted into the phone booth and sorted the change in his hand. He dropped the coin into the slot and dialed the number that he knew so well.

It's ringing, he thought to himself. Then, he heard the familiar voice say, "Hello."

"It's me," he said.

There was silence on the other end of the line.

"Hello, it's me."

There was still silence on the other end. Then, he heard…

"You can't come up. I know you're at the phone booth and you can't come up."

"I'll only stay for a little while."

"No. If you come up you'll want to spend the night and that is over."

"I just want to sit and talk for awhile, maybe drink a beer or smoke a joint."

"Look, you broke my heart too many times. It's over."

"Listen to me. I just want to talk"

"It's over. Just go home and leave me alone."

Click and then the dial tone. He dropped a coin into the slot and started to dial that familiar number and then he stopped. He hangs up the phone with a bang.

"Fuck!"

He ran to his car and fumbled with the keys.

"Goddamn it! I can't see."

He finally opened the door and jumped in. He shook his head like a wet dog. He rummaged around the car, trying to find something to clean off his glasses.

"My life is like a fucking country and western song," he muttered.

He sighed. He turned the key and started the car. He fiddled with the heat and defrost knobs, turned on the radio and opened a can of beer from a six-pack on the floor of the passenger side. He sat in the dark, sipping his Budweiser. He listened to Three Dog Night sing 'One is the Loneliest Number.'

He looked across the street. There's a homeless guy huddled in a doorway sipping from a bottle wrapped in a wet, brown paper bag.

"Thank God I'm not that guy."

A Hopeful New Journey

It is midsummer, hot. The day is half over. Three sweaty boys of fourteen sit on the steps with a basketball at their feet. Black, brown and white—their skin glistens in the sunlight. The brown boy has a red tank top on, but the black and the white boys are shirtless.

Charles, the black boy, has skin that is smooth and dark. His deep brown eyes are losing their youthful innocence, an adult squint of serious mistrust replaces the wide-eyed wonderment, but when he smiles his teeth shine and his eyes widen with kindness and humor.

Chuck, the white boy, is the skinniest of the three. He has short, light brown hair and pale blue eyes that seem to be in thought. There is a sprinkle of freckles across the nose and when he smiles his teeth never show. On his upper lip a faint shadow of young, sprouting whiskers that accents a cocky sneer which tries to tell the story, "even though I'm a skinny, pasty white kid, I can still be tough."

Carlos may be the handsomest of the three boys, only because his wavy black hair, even when unkempt, falls into place and always looks good. His mahogany brown eyes shine with the appropriate sparkle for every emotion. He has a childlike smile that is emphasized by one dimple.

The skinny white kid's hope is not to be like his father, a drunk that can't keep a job and can become mean even if he isn't drinking. He hopes for an education and to have someone to love him. His fear is that he'll become crazy like his mother, who supposedly ran off to Las Vegas.

The brown-eyed handsome one has hopes to become an actor, maybe someday a star.

His father laughs at such a dream, but his mother pinches his cheek and tells him that he is very handsome. He hides his fears deep within his charm.

The mistrusting one is very serious. He knows he is going to college. He already has good study skills and he reads things that he never tells his friends about. His fear is money. Where will he get the money?

They know how to stay away from trouble. They know how to be unseen. They're not gangbangers and they're not geeks. They're just fourteen-year-olds that live in the projects and play on the street, wise in some ways beyond their years. They are still concerned about Batman and willing to watch a Disney movie with a little brother and sister.

The big curiosity is, of course, girls.

What is the path to take? Which way to go? It seems so far away, but in four more years it will be their turn. College, the military, a job, Hollywood, jail, in love, loss of love or never to be held, a virgin, but you can never tell.

As children they live in the moment, free, letting their spirits soar. But to stay in the moment with eyes on the future is a hard thing to do, with questions of: Will success grace my path or will I give up? Will bad luck screw it up? Will I stay all mixed up?

Please tell me what's up. That's what they all ask the universe.

All three—Charles, Chucky and Carlos—have been friends since they were small boys. A trust binds their friendship and crosses over racial and cultural differences. But, now they are on a new journey, a journey that may separate them, a journey that will be dependent upon hope, a journey that will ask many questions and a journey that will define their destiny.

Each boy wants to be a man and each boy wants to be his own man. Each boy wants to keep their friendship as they journey into manhood.

The hope that we should have for all three boys is that they give hope to one another. Our prayer should be that they continue to help each other on their journey into becoming a man.

Thank You

To all the friends and family that encouraged and supported my writing.

To Charles Kiernan for his guiding wisdom.

To the Golden Gate Diner and their staff.

To Kristy Price, a very kind waitress.

A particular thanks to Dave "Fontaine" Howell, Bill "U.B." Carter, Marcella "M." Carter, Joe Molinari, and Blaine Hertzog.

A special thanks to Parisian Phoenix: Angel Ackerman, Gayle F. Hendricks, and Joan Zachary.

A continuous thank you to my lovely and beautiful wife, Barbara.

Larry Sceurman grew up in the Kaywin section of Bethlehem, Pa., in the 1950s and 1960s.

In his early teens, he worked with his grandfather in a small auto body repair shop where he observed that stories were a big part of the human experience. From vocational teacher to storyteller and now author, Larry has learned and shared the value of stories. He mixes truth and fiction to produce enjoyable, thought-provoking snippets of life.

Larry is influenced by the writings of Laura E. Richards, John O'Connor, Richard Ford, Michael J. Meade, Richard Rohr, and Billy Collins.

FICTION TITLES FROM PARISIAN PHOENIX

Also from Larry Sceurman:

The Death of Big Butch

May, 1974.
Jimmy Washburn, young family man, loses a good friend to a heart attack when only 27. The death teaches Jimmy about his community, friendship, and responsibility just in time for the birth of his second child. This debut novella from Larry Sceurman captures small-town Americana with humor and poignancy.

Trapped
By Seneca Blue
Photos by Joan Zachary

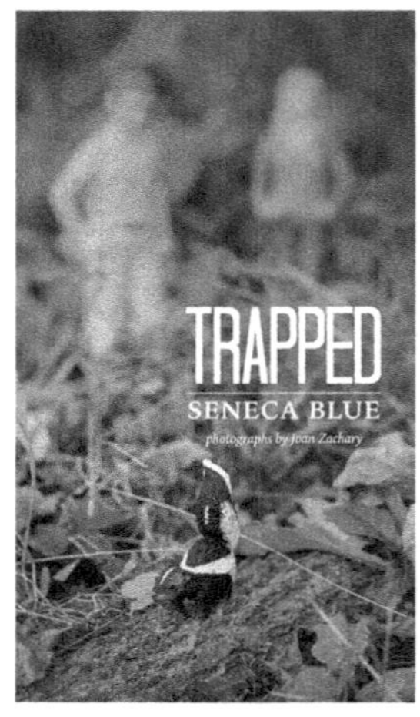

Trapped offers protagonists who are "real people" which was unheard of in the contemporary romance scene. The novel was written more than a decade ago featuring an overweight woman about to turn 40, overeducated and underemployed, which turned out to be a fascinating prognostication of the 2020 gig economy. This unique pocket book highlights the residents of Plastiqueville with stunning photos by Joan Zachary.

The Fashion and Fiends Series
By Angel Ackerman

Manipulations | Courting Apparitions | Recovery

Angel Ackerman's *Fashion and Fiends* series blends the suspense and fear of contemporary horror fiction with the humor and lightheartedness of late twentieth-century "chick lit." Her diverse network of characters experience the richness and depth of human struggle, which is why while the characters in the universe fall in love and pursue their happily-ever-after, the series can't quite be called paranormal romance.

Ackerman uses magic and the supernatural to explore weighted topics like domestic violence, body image and self-esteem, depression and grief, colonialism, women's rights, coming-of-age, religion, infibulation, infertility, and blended families. As Ackerman's characters navigate their world, they share the same plights their readers do.

Not The Quiet French Kid
By Angel Ackerman

Origin story for the protagonist, "Road Trip"

When Jules Zwiegenbaum moved from the South of France to the United States, he knew culture shock would be a problem. He was half-American, so how bad could it be? As a high schooler who loved to surf, California might suit him nicely. He even starts making friends. But when the school bully challenges him to a fight—it reveals a hereditary condition that Jules didn't know his family carried. Apparently, the abnormality prompted his parents' whole career as medical researchers in genetics. This is the story of how one young man learned about the inherited curse that links him to a world he thought only existed in fairy tales and horror movies.

NON-FICTION TITLES FROM PARISIAN PHOENIX

Stops Along The Way
By Charles Ticho

Charles Ticho—Czech born and a dual citizen of the United States and Israel—writes about his life in Europe, Israel and America, as a Holocaust survivor, film & commercial producer/director, world traveler and family historian. This memoir, published months before his death at 95, compiles many of his short essays, some new and some reworked from stories published in multiple global publications, including the *Jerusalem Post*. Ticho explores family, culture and Jewish history with his unique first person perspective.

TWISTS: Gathered Ephemera
By darrell parry

Webster's Dictionary defines Ephemera as, "something with no lasting significance."

The poems in this collection have been swept together from decades of open mics and feature performances, and pressed between these pages like fallen leaves like something fleeting, now preserved.

This book is the first full-length poetry collection from poet, artist and spoken-word performer Darrell Parry. Complete with nifty drawings and sage bits of wisdom scattered throughout, Twists offers a glimpse into a world of social anxiety and awkwardness with the experience and wisdom to accept an epic unknowing of everything.

**REVISED AND EXPANDED
SECOND EDITION NOW AVAILABLE**

Not an Able-Bodied White Man with Money:

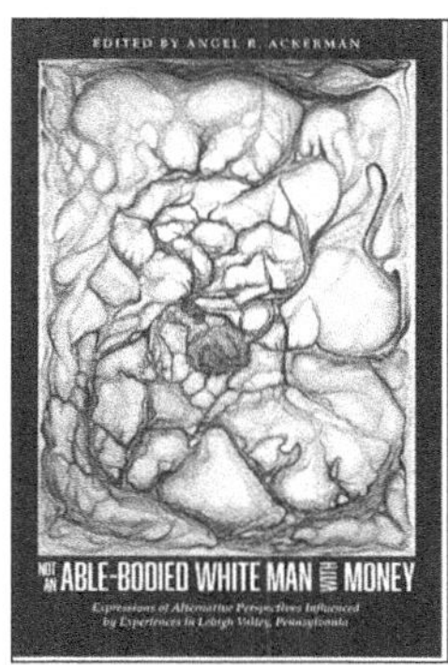

Expressions of Alternative Perspectives Influenced by Experiences in Lehigh Valley, Pennsylvania

Edited by Angel R. Ackerman

An identity politics anthology, *Not an Able-Bodied White Man with Money* features authors,poets, and artists selected not based on their writing ability, but for their ideas. The anthology features marginalized perspectives about LGBTQ issues, body image, disability, neurodivergence, ethnic backgrounds, mental health and much more.

The Phulasso Devotional

Engineering the Warrior Preist for Dark Times

Thurston D. Gill Jr.

This book balances spiritual and moral values with safety and security in a scary world.

Gill blends his experiences in law enforcement and Christian ministry, with his perspective as a security professional, to help others protect themselves and their loved ones in an emergency or situation. Also great for first responders.

Purchase our titles on our website, online or ask for them at your favorite bookseller.

DO YOU WANT TO HELP PARISIAN PHOENIX OR ANY SMALL PUBLISHER OR INDEPENDENT AUTHOR?

- Buy books. Buy more books. Give books as gifts.

- Recommend authors to friends.

- Share Social Media Posts.

- Leave a review:
  Amazon
  Goodreads
  Google Books

  - Readers use reviews to find books.

  - Retailers' web sites use reviews as part of their algorithm.

  - Some advertisers require a certain number of reviews.

- Join and share newsletters.

- Attend events.

- Join Goodreads and follow authors, mark their books as read, shelve and rate them.

- Check on Patreon and Kickstarter for the creators you love

- Start a book club.

Learn how 

Subscribe to our Newsletter, "Bookish Babble", on

substack

https://parisianphoenixpublishing.substack.com/